MURDER IN LIMA

MURDER IN LIMA

ROBERT A. LEVEY

CUTTING EDGE

ISBN-13: 978-1-962896-40-5

Published by
Cutting Edge Books
PO Box 8212
Calabasas, CA 91372
www.cuttingedgebooks.com

For Elsita
who thought she knew.

CHAPTER ONE

SWARMS OF SEAGULLS stole free rides on the fresh breeze over the docks of Callao, swooping down lazily for floating tidbits, and freighters tied up at the thick pilings rose on a slight swell. Mounds of packing cases stacked all over waited for the Monday trucks of Lima's busy import firms; recently lifted import restrictions had jammed the docks and warehouses with merchandise that had been out of sight for months. There was nothing really unusual about the scene if one over-looked the presence of a piece of mechandise that did not belong with the stenciled crates. It was a man's body.

A watchman making his rounds made the discovery and immediately came to the conclusion that it was either a case for the customs authorities or the police. Had it been alive, the corpse certainly would have been arrested for there were several PROHIBIDO FUMAR signs conspicuously posted about the place, and yet the corpse was surrounded by a litter of half-smoked cigarettes.

The undeclared merchandise was duly removed to the Central Morgue in Lima, a faded adobe building with scabby, peeling sides on Avenida Grau where several men, wearing stained frocks and hovering about the meat lockers, were ready with strong wrists and sharp scalpels to dissect it. The body, according to the wallet found in an inside pocket, once housed the varied talents of one Josef Barkovit, a native of one of several central European countries where Slavic tongues are spoken.

1

This could have made him Slav, Slovene, Croat, Serbian, Bosnian, or Czech. It really didn't matter. He was dead in any language.

I don't know what had induced me to come to Peru in the first place unless it was the letter from Enrique Leon, whom I had become friends with several years ago when I was covering the swimming pool set in Beverly Hills and he was taking some kind of a special course in the Police Academy of the Los Angeles Police. Leon was a member of Lima's *Guardia Civil,* the plainclothes or detective bureau. We had gotten together because of our mutual interest in criminology, and I don't mean the kind viewed with an infra-red camera through the keyhole of a Las Vegas motel, or filmed long-distance beside a suburban swimming pool.

Six years without a vacation was beginning to tell on me after being on an almost 24-hour routine of covering automobile trunk murders, yacht rapes and sudden departures caused by overdoses of sleeping pills. So I went to a place on Wilshire Boulevard that handles nothing but freighter trips. I had six weeks' leave with pay and certainly wasn't in any big hurry. They fixed me up on a nice Danish freighter which served food that the best eating places in Hollywood would have been proud of.

I made the 12th passenger on the list, which also included an old condor and his wife whose combined ages brought them back to G. Washington's time, a woman and three snotty monsters who wolfed down all the delicious Danish pastry at three o'clock every afternoon, a guitar-playing Panamaian who really knew how to play and had a good voice for his recently picked-up calypso songs, and finally a quartet of schoolteachers who had all the appearances of crawling out of an Arctic snowstorm and who were about as appealing as hunks of mastadon meat. But it was really quite a good trip, the food saving the day.

Leon met me at the docks and we got into a 1925 Packard which served as one of the local taxis or *colectivos.* Lima is about eight miles from Callao, the seaport, and is a mixture of antiquity and modernity. A few blocks away from comfortable hotels are walled adobe buildings with cedar balconies reflecting the Moorish influence that Spain brought to the New World. A couple of more miles took us to Miraflores, an attractive suburb of Lima, where Leon lived with his mother and sister, who with true Latin hospitality insisted I stay with them until I found an apartment of my own.

A good night's sleep can work wonders after two weeks on a rolling freighter, and although all night I still felt I was rolling, after a couple of cups of Peruvian coffee, *Cafe de Chanchamayo,* which Peruvians claim is the best in the world, I was ready for about anything, and it soon came.

"I know you just got here," said Leon, "but a man like you is used to a lot of activity and might get sick just doing nothing. This will be good relaxation for you."

I laughed. "What are you leading up to? A *muchacha* with long black hair and great big eyes?"

"Not this soon," said Leon. "This concerns a very unattractive man. Would you care to take a trip to the morgue this morning?"

I shrugged and said, "What have I got to lose except my breakfast, and I can always get another."

The part of the Central Morgue where the bodies were checked smelled like the men's room in a two-bit theater. I suppose the lavish use of disinfectants and preservatives was well warranted since some of the specimens weren't exactly fresh, and there were two which had been fished out of an alley near the Fisherman's Wharf in Callao that would have taken gallons of formaldehyde to make presentable for even a cursory examination.

It didn't take much of an examination to find that Barkovit had received an expert throttle job leaving him with a permanently broken neck and a slightly listing head, although aside from a slight bruise just above the collar and a purpling of the face, there was little to indicate to a layman that he had been the victim of anything more than a bad fall. The late Mr. Barkovit had a balding head, a long nose and a pair of glacier-blue eyes. He wore a flashy tie and sports jacket that carried the label of one of the better men's shops on Miami's Lincoln Road. A star sapphire, the size of a gallstone, flashed on the index finger of his right hand, and the gold in his mouth had made some dentist rich for life.

Barkovit, Leon told me, was a member of the "briefcase fraternity" that congregated at the El Rancho, a Peruvian facsimile of a Bavarian beerstube, complete to the dark paneling and beamed ceiling, old porcelain mugs with pewter lids, clouds of cigarette smoke and the stale smell of beer that had long sunk out of sight into the grimy tables and blackened floor. While the El Rancho was ostensibly a drinking place, food could be had and the spot was listed in the tourist guides as "the favorite meeting place for artists, writers and people of the theater."

The food specialty, for which it was supposedly famous, was *causa,* a salad concoction and a complete meal in itself, made with yellow potatoes mashed in olive oil and hot chili, seasoned with lemon juice and spices, several varieties of fish and shrimp, olives, cheese, eggs, corn on the cob and lettuce.

The "briefcase" boys dealt in all kinds of special sales work. Fugitives from countries dominated by Hitler's Third Reich, they made the El Rancho their headquarters, a sort of beery clearing house for merchandise of every description. Along with the food specialties, proposed plays and novels, it was a place for barters, deals, sales, contracts and general information. During World War II, a stream of commerce flowed from briefcase to briefcase until the cessation of hostilities put a crimp into the volume of the traffic. But it still went on.

An attendant at the morgue put Barkovit back into cold storage. Leon lit a cigarette. The smell of the strong black tobacco mingled with the nasal-drying fumes of formaldehyde.

"I think we have seen enough here," he said. "We have something to start with. Not much, but something."

"I feel like having a drink," I said. "Some good brandy. Maybe a couple of brandies. I'd like to forget Barkovit's face."

Leon grinned. "That is a good idea. We can go over to the El Rancho for a drink. I might even ask a few questions. Who knows? We may even get a few right answers."

"Porsupuesto, I knew him," said Jorge, the headwaiter at the El Rancho who was as old as some of the furniture in the place. He wiped the beads of condensation from a *poron* of beer with the edge of his dish apron and put it down on the table next to us. "He came here two, maybe three times a week. Did not like beer. Always had a glass of sweet vermouth. Never left me a *propina.* Big business man, bah!" Jorge threw up his hands.

"They found his car this morning," said Leon, "in one of those dusty parking lots off Huancavelica. It has probably been there for at least two days. The watchman does not seem to remember when it arrived or who brought it."

"What was it, small English auto, a Hillman?" asked Jorge, who was practically leaning on my shoulder.

"You will have to spend more money than that," said Leon. "Much more. It is a nice, sleek, yellow, convertible Oldsmobile. It now seems that this fellow was doing a larger business than most people thought. He even had me fooled. I didn't think he was such a big spender. But now that I think of it, I do remember seeing him breeze along Avenida Arequipa on two occasions. There was a girl with him both times but I didn't get a good look at her face. That was too bad. But I do know that Barkovit was friendly with Lisa."

Jorge was still listening. It is a good idea to tell the right kind of waiters what you want to know. They hear a lot of things that might be of value.

"You mean the *francesa* who ran the place where the Mexican strangled the Chilean girl?" he asked again.

"Francesa, my eye," said Leon. "A Pole would be nearer to describing her. She's been in every kind of business from Mexico

5

City to Buenos Aires and dozens of locations in Lima. Name any business and she's had her hand in it, the bad kind. If Barkovit knew her well then he was probably as rotten as she is and may have been working on something, although her place has been closed now for over two weeks since the case of *"La Mariposa de la Noche."* Don't you like that phrase? The newspapers really played it up. Anyway, we ought to drop in on Lisa and see what a lack of business has done to her disposition."

It was a pleasant ride towards Lima's suburbs. One enters the eucalyptus-lined Avenida Salaverry, and drives past the impressive statue of Jorge Chavez, Peru's intrepid airman, the first to cross the Alps. The spicy smell of the eucalyptus leaves filled the air near the Club Hipico, where Lima's riding enthusiasts came to see the horse shows.

Lisa's place on Calle General Ramirez was a bit different from the adjoining houses. In fact, it was a flower-covered bordella. A jacaranda tree with brilliant purple blossoms sprouted from the front lawn, and a vine flashing a profusion of orange flowers known locally as *"lluvia de oro,"* rain of geld, snaked to the roof and drooped over the doorway. Yellow oleanders flanked the front steps. It had all the romantic features of a love nest only in this instance the love wasn't so romantic. In Spanish, the house was *casa de tolerencia,* a term that certainly understates the house's function.

A dusky *cholita* opened a small aperture in the door and was about to slam it in my face when Leon said something to her in rapid Spanish. The downstairs was well furnished and in good taste with a number of comfortable chairs, attractive drapes, a fireplace that actually worked and a bar. The atmosphere was as homey as a men's club.

Lisa came downstairs and gave us a thorough looking over. She obviously knew Leon so her eyes spent more time searching me from head to foot. She wore a red and white flowered dress, that accentuated her obesity, and a small necklace of pearls, which considering her astuteness in the flesh trade, was probably authentic. She smoked a long cigarette and clutched a handbag to her spacious bosom as if she expected to be robbed.

She looked at me again and burst into a torrent of Spanish. I shrugged. Then she changed to broken English.

"What is to see me about?" she shrilled. "Is nobody here. My girls is go away. My business is finished." She grabbed a pile of papers on a tray and threw them on the table. I get nothing, only bills. I pay, pay, pay."

Her voice dropped several ocatves and she stared at me again. "Who is he?" she asked Leon.

"A friend of mine," he said.

"An American agent?"

"No," Leon laughed, "just a newspaperman."

"What is funny?" she asked. "I have many friends newspapermen. They know I am good friend to them. One time I have all directors from *El Diario* here. They real gentlemen. But now, I do not like foolish questions. The police have come here many times. What more you want now?"

"I am the police," said Leon, "and I'm not going to ask you any foolish questions. All I ask is a little information. What you do here is not my business. I am in another department. My business is murder. Understand? You knew Josef Barkovit. That is my business too."

Lisa began to get interested. She put out her cigarette and put down her handbag.

"You knew Barkovit," added Leon. He used to come here a lot and don't tell me he was a stranger. Of course, you know he is dead."

I was taking this all in. It was very interesting. I don't think that Lisa liked the look on my face.

She took a long cigarette from her bag. "Yes, I hear about it. How is it possible?"

"How is anything possible?" asked Leon. "That is what I would like to find out for myself. Just what did he do here, anyway?"

"He do like many of my good friends," said Lisa. "He bring people here for nice parties. Josef was very *simpatico*. He do me many favors."

"Like what?" asked Leon.

"Little things," she said. "Josef was always ready when I need him. You know how busy is things when business is good."

I could visualize what 'little things' Josef did for her, and they might have included blackmail, which wasn't hard to imagine considering the number of prominent people she knew.

"*Claro*," said Lisa. "I am friend to everybody. I am friend with police and big men in government. I have nothing to hide."

"Everybody's friend who has a stray dollar," said Leon on the way out. "Lisa appears to be cooperative but she has never fooled me. Did you get a good look at her eyes? They are scheming eyes. There is something behind them going on twenty-four hours of the day. I think she knows more about Barkovit than she pretends to know."

"She's a good actress but all of that commotion she created was just put on," I said. "It was even a bit on the hammy side. What do you think she will do now that the police have closed her place?"

"Don't worry about little Lisa," he said. "She has other hobbies. Perhaps better paying ones. And more luck than a cat has lives."

During the siesta, I decided to roam around town. The very first place to catch my attention was the *Maison de Arte* on Jiron Union which had several figurines in the window that reminded me of a few I had seen while roaming through Fritz von Papen's mansion during a brief lull after running halfway across Germany with one of Patton's taskforces. I had a good look at the things which were nicely displayed on red velvet and started to walk away when a man who did not look Spanish beckoned to me from the doorway.

"Come in," he said. "You are a friend of Enrique Leon, are you not?" And in the same breath: "Perhaps you are a detective, too."

I was really surprised. First, I hadn't been seen with Leon much as yet. Furthermore, this was supposed to be a country that insisted on very formal manners.

"No," I said, "just a newspaperman on a vacation. Besides, I'm not in a buying mood today."

"Please," he said. "A thousand pardons. I did not mean to be so rude pulling you in from the street in this manner. But could you do me a favor?"

I waited until Max Martellini introduced himself and squeezed out a small smile. He told me he was a Frenchman who had lived in Lima a long time, but he still looked and acted, for the moment, like the proprietor of a smart shop on Paris' Rue de la Paix.

"You are an American," he said, "and Americans have, shall we say, a certain touch for doing things expediently. I am sending an important letter to a large firm in New York, and there is the matter of spelling a word correctly and putting a phrase in such a way."

"All right," I said.

Martellini's office was up a flight of stairs over the shop. It had a thick rug, good furniture and even a small bar in the corner, and Martellini seeing me eyeing the bottles rushed over and quickly poured two drinks.

"I hope you like this brand," he said. "My brother ships me a few cases from his company in Bordeaux once in a while." The brandy was excellent.

Max had the letter half-typed in long, flowery phrases. Had he completed it, it would have covered at least three pages. I sat down and revised what he had written and added what else he had to say. The job took about twenty minutes and took up a single sheet, but it was an ordinary sort of letter, and the importance mentioned by Martellini seemed completely absent

Martellini looked over my shoulder and beamed. "Now you see what I mean." He ran back to the cabinet and refilled the glasses. Then he took the letter, signed his name at the bottom, folded it and put it into an envelope which he addressed in handwriting. He picked up his glass and settled back comfortably in his chair.

"Well, my friend, how do you find things here?"

"Interesting," I said. "I've just arrived on a vacation, and already I'm running around with Leon trying to dig up a few clues on a murder."

"Isn't that terrible!" said Martellini pausing over his glass. "How is Leon making out with the investigation? Does he have any information that may be of value in tracking down the murderer?"

Before Martellini could think of any more questions I said, "Leon is a policeman. There are a lot of things I don't think he would tell me, and I'm his friend."

"Of course," agreed Martellini. He extended his hand when I got up and I shook it. "Thank you very much," he said. "You have been most considerate."

"Not at all," I said, "and I admire your brandy very much. Thank you."

Martellini smiled. I got to the doorway in time to see Max peering at me from the corner of a window display. He wasn't smiling this time. In fact, he was frowning. I tried to add up things in my mind. The whole letter situation didn't make sense. I made a mental note to ask Leon about it when I met him this afternoon.

Continuing as a tourist I found that almost every street in downtown Lima has its groups of shops specializing in certain varieties of merchandise. This originated in the days when the city had areas that were identified by the items they sold. Thus today, parts are known as *los botones* (buttonmakers,) *los plateros* (silversmiths) and others. But on the narrow, lane-like streets leading to *El Barrio Chino* (the Chinese quarter) there is a hodgepodge of shops half-hidden among the worm-eaten cedar columns and crumbling walls of former residences in various stages of decay. Some of these are reached by arched doorways and courtyards paved with cracked and worn tiles in mosaic patterns that once reflected the sparkle from fountains long since dried out and now patinaed with streaks of weathered verdigris.

It takes a slow walker to see all of these places; dozens of narrow doorways can be overlooked by the man who sets a fast pace. After leaving Martellini, I had a couple of sandwiches and coffee and decided on a stroll to burn up the heavy Dutch cheese and the strong coffee. I walked leisurely, attracted by the pleasant odors that swirled from a cabinetmaker's shop where workers were planing freshly cut cedar and the spicy smell lingered in my nostrils.

Next to the cabinetmaker's shop was a room filled with a jumble of items that would have excited any antique seeker in the States. I can't resist old things, especially guns, and what caught my eye particularly was an old Martini-Peabody rifle, a Civil War surplus item that somehow found its way to Peru to be used in the disastrous and unfortunate War of the Pacific with Chile. The window had been freshly washed, a rare circumstance in this part of the city, and then the reflection of a more interesting object caught my eye.

It was a girl standing across the street staring at me and what a girl! Her glossy, jet black hair was cut in the current Italian style; she had beautiful teeth, large brown eyes and a body that was nothing but curves. Delicately pointed, her breasts were beautifully defined in a tight fitting black sweater.

I could see that she was trying to be obviously attractive which is not the usual state of affairs in Lima, at least not quite so publicly. She smiled as I crossed the street and said hello.

Her name was Graciela and she worked in a beauty salon just off the Plaza de Armes. Graciela said she had seen me this morning with Leon, who she knew casually. She spoke haltingly in English, which she said she had learned from a major in the Military Mission at the U. S. Embassy, and I believed her. This was her method of getting an introduction and I certainly didn't object. Although she said she liked Leon very much, she liked *Norteamericanos* much better. And, of course, she was always ready to improve her English.

We had some of that potent Peruvian coffee that sends your caffeine count soaring to new heights, and she never stopped talking, asking how long I'd known Leon, what I was doing in Lima and how long I expected to stay. She even got on the subject of the Barkovit murder, which was a big thing in the news, and asked if I thought that the police in the United States with their scientific methods would have already solved the crime.

"There's nothing wrong with the police here," I said. "Conditions may be different here but they operate along the latest lines. They will get to the bottom of the case soon, I'm sure. Things and life in general seem to move more slowly here, but what is the difference? They get there eventually."

"But the criminal may do more damage," she said slowly, practically spelling out each word.

"That's what the police run up against in any country," I said. "There are all kinds of possibilities that come up when they are looking for a criminal."

She mentioned Leon a couple of more times but didn't ask what he had found out up to the present time, which I was beginning to suspect she would do. Perhaps she thought I had told her everything that Leon had passed along to me. But she couldn't have asked questions any faster had she been reading from a prepared script. After I had finished, she decided to leave and said she would call me. She said it would be better that way, so I let it go at that But one thing was obvious. Our meeting had happened much too quickly. She could have been following me—she had come from the direction of the Central Market and she was not carrying a package.

I met Leon around three o'clock over some more coffee, and I told him about the meeting with Graciela.

"Good looking, isn't she?" remarked Leon. "Where did you find her?"

"In the *Barrio Chino*. But I think she found me. She was staring at me."

"How unusual," said Leon. "I know she talks a great deal but I didn't know she stared at men. And in the *Barrio Chino*, too. What a strange place for such an attractive girl. You are quite a wolf, my boy. Here you have been in Lima only a day and you already meet one of the most beautiful girls in town."

"Make it the other way around," I said. "She met me and really threw a bundle of questions around. What's new in the Barkovit murder so I can tell her the next time we get together?"

"I've got a lead but not for her," he said. "I was going through some files in the office and found out that he had been mixed up in some trouble at the race track here several years ago with a pal named Aranyi. That was while I was in the States. The files also had some testimony given by a Dr. Menada. Not much, but something, and the whole thing may have some bearing on the case. Anyhow we ought to get some more details from this Dr. Menada. Come along and we'll look him up."

The National Institute of Hygiene and Public Health on Avenida Salaverry looked like a big Moorish tomb from a distance. The place once belonged to a wealthy patron of the arts who made the mistake of siding with the wrong political faction and lent them his financial support. In a place where politics is a serious business, indeed, and where defeated candidates for high office and their more influential backers were given their choice of either being jailed or exiled, he got off easily. He was chastised and allowed to stay but his property was confiscated and the stables that once housed his prize race horses and polo ponies now contained big, fat nags, whose bloodstreams were used to store up anti-toxins, as well as rabbits, mice and guinea pigs for cancer research.

Dr. Menada, who was in charge of the place, had a good memory. Yes, he remembered Barkovit who had teamed up with a Hungarian named Aranyi and the veterniarian of the local horse track and had worked a lucrative business stimulating the horses. Nags that hadn't won a race in years had won big purses to the delight of the trio and the consternation of the astonished spectators. When the scheme was finally exposed, the veterinarian quietly resigned from his post, Barkovit and Aranyi were fined 10,000 soles and imprisonment. Barkovit beat the rap; Aranyi did not. The story ran in the papers for a few days until it became as interesting reading to the public as a dish of warmed-over cabbage.

"How about Aranyi?" I asked. "Where can we find him?" "You'll find him in his cell at the Fronton if you take the trouble to go over there. But it is not a very pleasant place to visit," the doctor replied.

But visit it we did. Peru has a coastline of some 1400 miles so it is not surprising to find seafood prominently indicated on the menus of Lima's best restaurants as well as in many of the places that run off Callao's waterfront which feature as their main course part of the catch brought in daily by the small fleet of boats. However, the Peruvian Alcatraz, rarely seen by traveling lovers of seafood, is completely unadvertised in eating circles and does not even go to the trouble of printing a menu. Off the tourist beat, this spot is the Peruvian Alcatraz on desolate Fronton, a fog-shrouded rock most of the year, that lies a couple of miles out of Callao. The clientele is made up of bad guessers who chose the wrong political party, homosexuals and other varieties of the middle sex, and a few murderers doing stretches for "crimes of passion" which are not regarded with as much magnitude in Peru as they are in English-speaking countries and whose perpetrator rarely gets a life sentence. The inmates have the run of the place to the water's edge, and even have the privilege of going fishing if they so desire. But it is distinctly against league rules to use a boat.

After checking in with the Ministry of Government and Police, we wound up with a sheaf of papers covered with seals and signatures, and a special pass for me, being a foreigner, stating that my political views were not concerned with Peruvian affairs, that none of my friends or relatives were guests on the island, that my visit was strictly impersonal and impartial and that I would not reproduce for publication any description of conditions I happened to encounter.

A friend of Leon's at the Callao Boat Club fixed us up with a home-made cockleshell boat and by four-thirty we were chugging for the rock.

On one side, the current ran through a narrow opening in a row of sand bars with the speed of a millrace meeting huge swells that almost made me sick. It was a good sign to see the mussel boats which meant the island was close by—they got the shellfish from the black, jagged rocks near the penal colony. The rocks were covered with thousands of cormorants and gulls and their shrill cries were combined with the hoarse barks of the sealions that surfaced occasionally.

We were met at the dock by three soldiers carrying bayonneted Mausers who nodded in recognition and even saluted Leon. Another soldier, a sergeant, took our papers to an office with the name of a lieutenant painted on the door. He returned in a few minutes with a big signature scrawled on all the papers and told us where we could find Aranyi.

Farsac Aranyi was a gaunt, slight Hungarian with a pencil line mustache. Aranyi didn't need any urging to talk. He seemed glad to see us and talked all the time. Occasionally there was a break in his conversation when he coughed.

"My lungs," he said. He pointed to the moisture condensing on the walls, then tapped his chest. "That is bad for me here."

Aranyi coughed again and covered his mouth with a handkerchief. "I will leave here soon. I am going to be pardoned. Just six more months and I will go to the mountains and work for a friend who has a farm. Maybe the air will make me better.

"So Barkovit is dead," mused Aranyi after a moment "Was it a woman who did it?"

"We don't know yet," said Leon, "although the evidence indicates that *a* man did the job. It would take a very strong woman to break a neck the way Barkovit's was."

"I had a few business deals with Josef," said the Hungarian. "But I never liked him. He was always looking for what Americans call an angle." He pronounced it hangle. "A few times he spoiled some good possibilities because he was too greedy. So I finally got tired of his methods and left him." He didn't mention that he had left under armed guard. "Barkovit must have made plenty of money at the El Rancho during the war. They were big money years. Have you seen Lisa Morel? Barkovit was always hanging around her place when he wasn't at the El Rancho."

"Did she know him well?" asked Leon.

"Very well, I should say," said Aranyi. "He was her brother-in-law."

"Brother-in-law?" said Leon. "That's a new development. Lisa didn't say a thing about that. Maybe she figured that now the guy is dead and his usefulness to her is over, she didn't want to talk too much about him. On the other hand, she may be covering up something. Maybe she didn't think Barkovit was as nice as she said he was."

"Are you going to question her as to why she didn't tell you about her relationship with Barkovit?" I asked.

Leon shook his head. "No, I have a better idea. I'm going to keep a good eye on her from now on."

When I got back to the apartment that I'd found just before dinner, I found a note waiting for me at the switchboard downstairs. It added up to Graciela Salinas. She must have gotten my number from Leon's mother, and she must have been waiting for me with the phone in her lap because she answered .in the split second the first ring started.

"Allo, Roberto," she said in a smiling voice, "what are you doing tonight?"

"Not a thing," I said. "Just got back from a boat trip and can get the salt out of my hair in fifteen minutes. Are you lonely tonight?"

"I am always lonely," she said, "especially for men with green eyes. You will come tonight, soon? I will be watching for you from window."

This was one invitation I was not going to pass up even though it had been a very full day. I changed my clothes and downed a quick brandy. Graciela was something special, the kind of a *muchacha* the Peruvians, or anyone for that matter, called well constructed, and in my opinion she had a little more than just looks.

Graciela lived in a small *casita* in Miraflores with her mother, who was conveniently taking in a movie at one of the local *cines,* and she was standing in the doorway the moment my footsteps sounded on the flagstone walk.

She looked even better than she had this afternoon in the Chinese Quarter. I don't know the reason why black looks so attractive on good-looking, well-built women, but on Graciela it was terrific. Black and just the right touch of gold jewelry. Curves covered in black and gold.

"Buenas noches," she cooed. She reached back and smoothed a little tendril of glossy black hair and motioned me towards a sofa and a table that had a couple of drinks ready.

"I knew you would be here on time," she said. "You *Norteamericanos* are so *en punto* and I like that. I make some capitans. You like?"

"Sure, I like," I said. But that was before I almost choked on the first one. Graciela certainly made them potent. Just about seven parts of pisco to one of vermouth, a quick atomizer spray of vermouth. It appeared that the nice looking *muchacha* with the beautiful legs and sensational body was out to get me stinking drunk, quickly, although all *gringos* are supposed to be heavy drinkers so perhaps she was only following a generally accepted pattern. While I don't have any aversion to getting drunk in the right company, I didn't want to miss any of this evening.

Graciela sipped her drink slowly. I felt like reaching over and taking her glass. I'd have bet it was straight vermouth. She put her glass down and fitted her body into the corner beside me.

"How do you like Lima," she asked.

"Good, very good," I said.

"And the women?"

"*Simpatica*," I said. "Very *simpatica*."

She smiled. The women in Lima all like to hear that phrase from foreigners, I've been told, and it looked like I'd told her just what she wanted to hear. She put her hand on my shoulder.

"And me?" she asked, coyly making her large brown eyes even larger.

"Wonderful," I said. "Ever since this afternoon, I've been thinking about nobody but you. I've been longing to see you so much that I haven't been able to sleep. Been taking sleeping tablets. Look at my eyes and see how heavy they look."

She looked into my eyes all right and when she met me eye to eye some kind of perfume with a low melting point swirled up into my head. Her arms went around my neck and she kissed savagely. She moved back to appraise the effect and then kissed me again. Graciela was more active than Vesuvius in mid-July, and she didn't need any alcohol to stoke her furnace. Graciela half-pulled me up from the sofa and maneuvered me towards the bedroom leaving a trail of black and gold that ended at her bed.

The bed was comfortable and after Graciela I began to doze. My blissful state didn't last very long. The telephone rang with a piercing sound and Graciela sprang out of the bed.

She came back into the bedroom in a couple of minutes. "My mother," she said. "She will be returning soon so you must go. You are very good."

"We must see each other more," I said. "Mind if I tidy up a bit before I go?"

"Oh, no," she said and pointed to the direction of the bathroom.

I ran the water and combed my hair and dabbed at the lipstick smirches that ran down the back of my neck. I don't know how much time I spent in erasing the marks of the encounter but when I looked out of the doorway I could see Graciela stealing past the door. Leaving the water running, I tip-toed into the bedroom and put my eye close to the partially opened door. My coat was still hanging on the chair where I had left it after peeling off to escape the heat from the first drink, and the *muchacha* was rummaging through my pockets with all the dexterity of a pickpocket, even feeling along the seams to find out if I had a stray dollar tucked away for a rainy day. Outside of a couple of hundred soles, about ten bucks in American money, my wallet contained the usual junk one carries around. I had jotted down a few interesting facts about Lima, had a press card issued by *El Diario,* some clippings about a jungle expedition operating in the province of Madre de Dios that Leon had given me and a photo taken with a girl at Laguna Beach. Not much of a take.

What Graciela was looking for she apparently didn't find, and I could see a mounting expression of disappointment color her face as she replaced the wallet in the coat.

I went back into the bathroom and shut off the water, whistled a few notes and walked slowly back to the living room.

Graciela was not a very good actress. She was a perfect picture of complete frustration but tried to hide her feelings by smiling wanly. Her eyes still looked angry as she took me by the arm and practically rushed me out of the house.

"Please," she said, "my mother will be here in any moment. You must go now. But I will call you again, yes?"

CHAPTER TWO

L EON WAS AT my apartment by eight the next morning. "Well, my friend," he said after I'd made coffee, "and how did you amuse yourself last night?"

I told him, and his eyebrows flew up, Then he tossed the morning paper he'd brought with him across the table to me.

"They fished her out of the river at two o'clock this morning. You didn't kill her with kindness last night, did you?"

"Come off it!" I protested. "I left her at ten o'clock and came straight home."

He reached over and patted me on the back. "Don't worry. I know you didn't do it but it is lucky that you are a good friend of mine. Ordinarily, you would be in jail as a suspect until you were cleared. But, of course, I will vouch for you." He winked. "You will be in my custody."

"She got a phone call when I was there," I said. "She said it was from her mother, and that she was coming home any minute."

Leon shook his head. "Her mother was out of town visiting relatives in Arequipa."

"Then it must have been the murderer who called," I said. "At least somebody she knew. They must have had something to talk over. That's why she wanted to get me out of the house in such a hurry."

'That's possible," said Leon, "but she wasn't killed in the house. The place was in perfect order when we examined it. Only the bed was unmade. There would have been some signs of a struggle if she had been murdered there. No, she must have met somebody at the bridge. She was dead before she was thrown into the river. Strangled. The water is rough this time of the year coming down from the mountains. Her body was wedged among the rocks, and it took quite a battering. Her face was not good to look at."

Leon looked at his watch. "I'm going to Headquarters now and get together with the boss. He has an idea that the same guy who killed Barkovit killed Graciela Salinas. Same technique. I'm inclined to agree with him. Tell you what I'll do. Meet me in front of the *Cine* in an hour. They are showing a film based on actual cases from the files of the Los Angeles Police. We might get some ideas."

It was 9:15 when I glanced at my watch, a good half hour before the picture went on and plenty of time for a smoke. I picked out a marble bench in the Plaza, in back of the statue of General San Martin partially surrounded by high shrubbery which kept the spot out of the direct sunlight. My cigarette was half-finished when my neck felt skewered by an icepick, both sides of my throat were stuck together and the General and his horse whirled towards me at a terrific speed, exploding in a blinding light.

When a high pitched voice kept stabbing at my brain, becoming louder and louder, I found myself staring into a small face which shaped itself out of the mist, picking up two bright black eyes and a pigtail as it became clearer. A small hand then appeared thrusting a ragged bit of paper a few inches from my nose.

"*Un mil soles,*" said the voice, "*Lima-Callao, hoy dia. Un mil soles, Senor.*"

I tried to say something but my tongue was stuck to the roof of my mouth. I probably looked just like the host of pisco imbibers who had found the benches scattered about the Plaza good spots to sleep it off. I felt my . inside pocket for my wallet. It was still there. I gave the little girl some money and stuffed the dog-eared lottery ticket into another pocket and leaned back to get the feel of the cold marble on the back of the neck. The big Braniff clock showed exactly eleven o'clock. I got up shakily and side-stepped my way to one of the cafes near Carabaya. The coffee was strong enough to jolt back into place any displaced vertebrae. A couple of cups might have revived a partially embalmed body. Then I met Leon. Just as the show was letting out.

"Where have you been, amigo?" he asked. "You are a fine one boasting that you never fail to keep an appointment."

"I usually do if I'm not waylaid," I said. "Take a look at the back of my neck. I'll bet it looks like a sunset over Lake Titicaca."

Leon whistled loudly. "You're right! It is green, black, red and blue. A little harder and your head would have rolled right into the lap of one of the waiters in the Palermo Restaurant across the street."

"Maybe the same guy who knocked off Barkovit and Graciela Salinas is trying to scare me off because I'm a friend of yours. Nobody tried to rob me. There wasn't a thing taken from my wallet."

"See anybody around who might fill the bill?"

"How could I with this mob of lottery ticket sellers milling around the place?" I said. A spasm of pain ran up my spine and I rubbed my neck vigorously.

"You'd better go home and lie down," said Leon. "If your neck bothers you, I'll call a doctor."

"Thanks," I said, "but I think I can take care of things. It's just a little worse than a bad hangover." I pulled out a handkerchief to wipe the beads of perspiration from my forehead. The coffee was starting to work on my deadened nerves. The lottery ticket I had bought from the street gamin fluttered to the ground.

Leon picked it up. "A thousand soles. That would be around fifty bucks in American money. Not bad for a few centavos. Just think, if you were with me you would have missed the opportunity of a chance to win all this money. Don't forget to look at the newspapers tomorrow, and I'll bet you'll find yourself with an extra thousand soles. Money like that can come in handy."

"Sure," I said wryly.

Leon laughed. "Go home and lie down. Stay around the apartment. I'll see you later."

By a little after noon I had forgotten about Leon's suggestion to stay in the apartment and take it easy. A hot bath and a trio of brandies fixed me up and I felt like a new man. The rubber had gone out of my legs and I felt restless. The only hangover I had was thinking of how alive Graciela had been last night and how dead now. Some fresh air would do me some good. I put on a clean shirt and ran my fingers over my face. I needed a shave. The only drawback was that I was fresh out of both blades and shaving cream.

The nearest place open was the Farmacia Inca, in the Barrio Rimac, over the bridge. Once you cross the bridge, you are in another city as far as the appearance of the place suggests. Once the best part of Lima, it contained the mansions of the viceroys and the house built by Viceroy Amat for the dancing girl Perricholi that was still standing. The red and blue sign over the drugstore flashed in the sunlight. A moldy smell of damp earth permeated the air coming from the walls of crumbling adobe buildings where pieces of plaster had fallen away exposing strips of bamboo and layers of reeds stuck together with chopped straw and dried mud.

Not long after getting what I wanted at the *farmacia*, where one could also get a shot of penicillin for an impending cold, get his tonsils swabbed or get advice for an abortion, it didn't take long to discover that I was being followed by three *hampones*, or local thugs or bums. I heard the word *gringo* mentioned a few times and decided that I had to move quickly. I walked faster and so did they, giving me a good look at the trio which included a tall, skinny bird with dirty cotton pants and an oversized striped short sleeved shirt that hung on him like a scarecrow. His legs must have been six feet long, and he let go with one of them that caught me on the side and the pain ran right up to my ears. The other two moved closer and I expected to wind up in one of the stinking alleys between the moldering houses.

The sun gleamed on the polished body of a police car as it suddenly rounded the corner and my assailants melted into an arched doorway. I didn't wait to discover where they had gone and turned quickly toward the bridge. When I got back to the apartment, I gulped down a fast brandy.

But Leon roared with laugher when, over lunch, I told him what had happened. "I told you to stay home. If you needed a few blades, I could have gotten them for you. I told you that I was coming back, didn't I?"

There was nothing to do but admit that he did. Leon took me by the arm. "Do you feel all right?"

"A little jumpy but not too bad," I said.

"Good!" he said. "I have a treat for you at Headquarters."

By two o'clock we were waiting for the line-up at the *Prefectura,* which houses the *Cuerpo de investigación, Vigilancia e Identificion,* otherwise the Peruvian FBI, which was just in back of the Central Prison for Men. Headquarters was a pale yellow stucco building with shady gardens where blackboard sessions for the police were held daily by instructors. It was ideally located. Those who failed to make a good impression at the lineups had only to walk across the lawn and pick out a straw mattress in the jail and prepare themselves for at least another evening inside the red brick hostelry.

There was an almost hourly bag of riff-raff in town and Leon suggested that we look into the place and take a chance that we might meet up with the thugs who gave me a bad time in the Barrio Rimac. The office of the Director General was on the first floor, a small cubbyhole containing a desk, filing cabinet, a few chairs, a bench and a heart-warming collection of bums beaming down from most of the walls. In the back of the desk was a glass covered case containing a collection of knives, guns, bludgeons and ropes, all accessories carried by gentlemen out for pleasant strolls.

Raymondo Salin de Moran, the Director General, lit a *presidents* and the heavy pungent smell of black tobacco filled the small room. He shook Leon's hand and then mine.

"It is a pleasure to have a visitor from *Los Estados Unidos*, especially at what you call line-up time. I think you will find our company very interesting."

Leon explained why we had dropped in and told Moran about the two assaults made on me.

Moran smiled. "Perhaps you should take out 'attack insurance' and make Leon the beneficiary and everything will work out nicely."

"Thank you," said Leon.

"That may be a good idea," I said, "but in the meantime if I get another crack on the neck and a good kick, I'll wind up as soft as a dish of tapioca pudding."

I didn't think the remark was exceptionally funny but it seemed to tickle Moran's funny bone and he let out some lusty bellows. "You are most amusing, my friend. I shall have to take good care of you."

Moran got up from his desk. He was squat and powerfully built like a wrestler. I was glad to have him on my side. "Come, the visitors will soon be here," he said. "This way, please." He opened a door and pointed to a row of seats that faced a whitewashed wall.

"Wait until you see what comes out," said Leon. "Sometimes it is even better than watching a movie."

They soon came out, a disreputable looking crew of characters that would have made a good cast for a documentary on the various social levels in the criminal structure of society. A file of *rateros* (pickpockets), *hampones* (thugs), and *ladrones* (just ordinary thieves) turned their backs to the wall and faced us.

"Aren't they an attractive group?" asked Leon, "and so accommodating, too. They would do almost anything if you paid them well enough."

All of them had nicknames since it was considered bad taste to be called by one's real name. One was known as *cabeza de melon* (melonhead), another *el Chino* (the Chinaman), a third *ninito* (the kid), and another *cara de perro* (dogface). As they looked our way, a late arrival came in. He was called *el cuchillo* (the knife) and the appellation fitted him perfectly. A scar ran from ear to ear.

Melonhead looked the part of a congenital idiot as he leaned forward on one leg, letting his head rest on his shoulder and smiling and licking at a stream of saliva that drooled from the side of his mouth.

"Don't let that performance fool you," said Moran. "Some of these *gallinazos* are good actors. This one has been arrested a dozen times picking pockets on the streetcars. He is a specialist in that field. I am sure that if he saw me sitting here he would not waste his act."

There were three more line-ups of the unwashed and the place began to smell like a hole occupied by ditchdiggers on a hot day. Even Moran, who was used to such company, noticed the change in the air and lit a cigarette to cover up the aroma. But there was not a trace of any one of the trio. They were probably well holed up someplace in the Barrio Rimac waiting for a favorable time to emerge.

"Did you see any of your friends here?" asked Moran.

I shook my head.

"Never mind," he said, patting me on the shoulder, "most of them turn up here sooner or later. They are not as smart as they think they are and have to make a mistake." He held up a finger. "One little mistake is all that is necessary."

Pepe Romano was apparently "number one" boy about town and was affectionately known to the female population of Lima, both single and married as *El Lobo de Lima*. He was a tall, good looking fellow, exuding plenty of masculine charm, with brown, wavy hair and a toothy smile that was well advertised in the coffee shops, sidewalk cafes and night clubs he frequented. Romano was referred to as a dynamic businessman by the local tabloids who magnified everything he did and usually photographed him behind the wheel of a stripped-down, hopped-up, Ford coupe advertising the qualities of a brand of motor Oil and a car battery of which the firm he worked for was the sole distributor in Peru.

When the road racing season was on, Romano's name always headed the list of entrants. He never won a race; the best he could do was tenth place one year; but at least he was photogenic and the girls screamed when he waved his yellow scarf on the first lap of the Lima-Trujillo grind. But the race started tomorrow at nine, and Romano was working overtime to get his rattletrap in condition for the rugged contest that invariably left the sands along the Pan-American Highway littered with parts of vehicles and unfortunate drivers.

By four that afternoon we approached the flat adobe building that was once a residence in the gilded age of the Spanish viceroys. Romano's office was at the end of a maze of refrigerators, tractor accessories, tires and electrical appliances. We had to negotiate an obstacle course to reach Pepe's desk which was covered with loose files, which judged by their layer of dust were little used, and an overflowing wastepaper basket which probably held his correspondence. Romano was pecking away at a typewriter, one finger at a time, and looked up as Leon knocked over a pile of cans of motor oil that was supposed to be a floor display.

"Just finished a big deal," he said to Leon in Spanish. "My boss should give me a bonus and a month's vacation for this."

"Meet a friend of mine, Bob Johnson," said Leon.

"Hi, pal," said Romano. He had spent a few years with a petroleum company in California (his firm carried their products) and his English was pretty good. "Just in time for a drink."

Romano reached back on a shelf and took a bottle with a label printed *Pisco Puro de Ica.* "Best in Peru," he said. "Naturally, we are the sole distributors for the country. The distillers would not trust anybody else but ourselves since you know there are people who would dilute this product. Can you imagine anybody being so dishonest as to spoil the flavor of this marvelous drink?"

For the sake of convention, I had to down a shot of the most fiery stuff that ever maligned the fair name of the grape, diluted or undiluted. Tears came to my eyes and I gasped for breath.

"Wonderful stuff!" exclaimed Romano smacking his lips. "Wonderful!"

Romano put down his glass. "Well, gentlemen, what brings you here this afternoon?"

"Bob would like to see you shoot those scenes at Pachacamac," said Leon. "He's interested in documentary films like you have been making. After all, he is from Hollywood."

"Of course, of course!" said Romano. He had been really flattered. "Always glad to have somebody with us who is interested in our technique. Tell you what! Come out to the set around 8 tomorrow. You'll see everything."

After we had that settled, I went with Leon to his mother's house where we had dinner and a couple of drinks afterward. But I went home early, thinking that I'd done more running around and getting beaten up in Lima in two days than would have been possible in LA in two weeks.

CHAPTER THREE

P ACHACAMAC IS A pre-Inca run that can be seen from the Pan-American Highway as it knifes its way through yellow desert sands south of Lima. Most of what was once a city of considerable size was now blunted heaps of rubble but part of the place had been reconstructed by the government, and it was here that Romano had decided to shoot some scenes.

Pepe really surprised me with two truck loads of costumes and props, Lima starlets, Rimac Airline hostesses fast on the comeback, especially a British babe named Patty Parsons, who hailed from Montevideo and had an answer for everything, and a couple of well-built Peruanos who took care of the pool at the exclusive Palomar Beach Club and were standard fixtures in the innumerable beach parties that take place in the isolated little coves that dot the Peruvian coast.

A wizened little Japanese scurried out of a truck carrying a camera and tripod that was bigger than he was and wiped off the lens which was covered with a fine film of desert dust. The Temple of the Sun was selected for the first scene and the girls and assorted characters melted behind a pile of crumpled adobe huts to get into their costumes. Above us, facing the sea, loomed the Temple of the Moon, but Pepe decided that our present spot was better, and the rest of the equipment was unloaded.

Romano was producer, director and all-around technical staff for a recently formed movie company which was specializing in documentaries on Peru. As Pepe obviously didn't have the cash to launch the enterprise, somebody else did and Leon furnished the particulars. The money had been supplied by Maria Camargo, the darling of the Mexican films, probably revenue from nicely situated pieces of real estate in Mexico City, Acapulco and other locales. I had seen Maria on the screen and she really was all they advertised her as being.

A cream-colored Jaguar pulled up in a cloud of dust and in the distance a few additional cars belonging to tourists began to move up to where the scenes were going to be shot. Maria Camargo pulled her long legs over the long, sleek body of the car. She wore a low cut white blouse pulled loosely about her shoulders, a swirling flowered skirt and big gold loop earrings. Maria was well filled out, not stocky, but tastefully rounded. Her face was framed by a mass of dark red hair which seemed to match her eyes. Maria had the kind of pleasing attractiveness that would keep a long time.

"Hello, doll!" said Romano rushing up and kissing her hand. "What a big surprise having you here!" He kissed her hand again. Romano certainly knew what he was doing considering all the money she had sunk into the deal, and he was falling all over her in a demonstration of how he felt. Maria had a face and a figure that merited more than a second glance and Pepe looked as though he were going to wind up with both Maria and her money.

Romano introduced us. "How are things in Las Vegas?" she asked. "I haven't been there for over three years."

"The tables are still humming," I said. "The prices of the motels are going up but they still do the business. Then, of course, you can go to Reno and get the same thing."

"Or even Tijuana," she reminded me. She looked around. "I hope those tourists don't scratch their initials on my car. I only bought it last week."

A man and his fat wife had come over and examined the props minutely and poked about the piles of adobe bricks probably thinking there were stray gold pieces at the bottom. You can always tell the American tourist in Peru. The men carry more equipment than is featured in some photographic shop windows and the women—you can almost tell to a day when they arrived by counting the number of flea bites that show up painfully through their nylons.

A beachwagon pulled up to where the prop trucks were parked. "Excuse me a minute," said Romano, "that must be Dulantro with the sound equipment. I'll be back soon."

One of the girls in the cast appeared in the doorway of the Temple of the Sun wearing a colorful costume that was no doubt a duplicate of one on display in the textile section of the National Archaeological Museum.

The fat woman studied her intently. "Do you think she *is* an Inca princess, Dad?"

"I don't know, Mother," he replied, taking off his straw hat and wiping his brow. "There must be some around here yet. This is Inca country, you know."

Maria nudged me and winked. "If you were in costume I'm sure they would think you were Atahualpa, the last of the Inca emperors."

"Not with this face," I said. "You're thinking of another production."

"You're not too bad looking in a rugged sort of way," she said, looking at me with an arched coyness.

"Weatherbeaten would be a better description," I said.

Maria Camargo put her hands on her hips. "Let me see, you are about five feet, eleven inches tall, have most of your hair, good teeth, weigh about 175 pounds and your nose is a little off to one side."

"I got that nose from a motel customer who didn't like the questions I asked him. His left hand was too fast for me to follow."

She turned on her heel and watched my face in profile. It looked even worse that way.

Romano came up to us on a trot even though it was going to be a warm day. The "Mexican Bombshell" and I had been conversing just long enough for Pepe to get worried about his girl in the company of a stranger.

Pepe gave me a look that said, "Hands off, that's my property!" and gave her arm a pinch that I suspected was deeper than it appeared. Maria reddened and I expected Pepe to get a good resounding belt that would have set him back on his heels. But nothing happened and we walked back to the ruins where the last scene of "The City of the Emeralds" was going to be filmed.

After the last shots, Pepe Romano became very chummy. He discovered that I had an even less than casual interest in Maria Camargo, so he rewarded me for my pure intentions with an invitation to a lunch, as his guest, in a big house in San Isidro hidden behind dense hedges of arborvitae and jupiter.

The place was headlined by the blonde, bosomy, Scots-born wife of an Austrian representative of a French machinery company who had more data about what was going on in Lima behind her wheat colored-hair than all of the local correspondents of the AP, the UP, the INS and the cigar smoking boys with their feet up on the desks in the U. S. Embassy. Hetty Telger's bosom was extravagantly displayed in a low cut dress, and I could see she was well pleased with the attention it received. Her high complexion, which went beautifully with her hair and everything else, was not acquired in the highlands of Scotland, I learned, but in the high Andes, where her father had been the superintendent of a copper mine.

Over glasses of benedictine and brandy, Hetty imparted more news about Lima during day and night than Elsa Maxwell knew about New York and The Duchess. I don't know why Hetty had singled me out of the crowd to talk to except perhaps that I was the only new arrival there. But she said that she liked to talk with men who had green eyes. Invariably, most of them were interesting. Some, she said, were even dangerous.

Hetty's house was a roost for an unusual assortment of birds. There was a high ranking naval officer and his already inebriated wife, who reached through her alcoholic haze and thrust both hands to the elbow through a big cake covered with whipped cream and proceeded to devour huge chunks until scuttled by her irate spouse, who rushed her to a back room; an ex-Nazi engineer who kept his ears cocked throughout lunch with the anticipation of a terrier expecting a ham bone; a Peruvian doctor with the Cesar Romero look; and an American schoolteacher with a bull-dog face, who upset all the theories commonly associated with the womanly teaching profession in her complete lack of reticence about marriage. She had been wed three times and was looking for a fourth husband and was definitely not the sort recommended for a boy's school.

There was also a lady dude-ranch owner from Arizona with hair dyed the most god awful shade of funereal black. With it went a weathered face and bright orange lipstick.

The doctor with the Cesar Romero look spoke no English but understood plenty. He had a very appropriate expression for the lady with the raven hair. He called her a *polilla* and she beamed when she heard it.

"*Polilla*, what's that?" she asked. "I suppose it's something nice." She smiled at the doctor and pushed back a stray wisp of black thatch.

But she didn't know the word was Spanish for a moth and there were a lot of subdued snickers in the background.

The moth talked incessantly about her late husband. "Fred had such lovely eyes. And he was such a big fellow, six feet, six. He had a heart condition and didn't know about it for a long time. When he found he hadn't long to live, he wanted to leave his eyes to an eye bank. But I wouldn't allow anybody to have Fred's big, lovely brown eyes."

Fred's eyes never reached the eye bank. The moth rented a crop dusting plane when he cashed in and scattered his ashes all over the desert. And now she too was looking for another husband.

Hetty had evidently heard enough about Fred's eyes and urged me into a corner of the patio which was hung with rows of lanterns over clumps of bougainvillaea and oleander. By this time, her husband was well engrossed in conversation over the merits of his water-well drilling equipment with a group of hacienda owners, since water is a precious thing on the arid coast where the big money crops of cotton and sugar are raised.

She put a disc on a record player, a slow samba (I think it was called either a *bahia* or a *bayon*) and we danced to the music which was mostly a flute rendition with a background of drums, the kind of music you could dance to all afternoon, especially with the odor of flowers in your nostrils and something solid in your arms.

Hetty had wide shoulders and a bosom that welled up to her collarbone. She was tall, almost as tall as I, but she moved about with lithe steps that made her feel almost feathery. She dug her fingers into my shoulder and held on tightly with her other hand. I got the impression right away that she was not a person to be trifled with unless you were prepared to go the limit.

"You're very good," she said. "Do you like this kind of music?"

"Love it," I said. "A couple of more brandies and more of this tempo and I'd be ready for anything."

She dug her fingernails deeper into my shoulder. "We must do this more often. My husband hates to dance, says it is a waste of time. Besides, he's always busy with people who drop in." She looked at me. "Machinery is such a dull subject."

I agreed, but soon had to apologize for having to cut our somewhat more interesting conversation short because I had to meet Leon at the bullfights.

This Wednesday afternoon was a big day in Lima, for it ushered in the bull fight season, the time of the year when Limenos went into hock to scrape up enough money for the performances.

The program included four of the spectacles which ran on successive weeks and only the well-heeled could afford tickets for all four, in the best locations, of course, the cost of which ran in the neighborhood of thousands of soles. A lot of grocery clerks and bank tellers had little to eat but rice and beans the day after a bullfight, but they were happy. They had something to talk about for a long time. The few who saw all four fights probably had a lot less to eat, but after all, the bullfights came only once a year.

The Lima bullring was located on Avenida Venezuela on the way to Callao and was known as the *Nueva Plaza de Toros de Lima* to keep tourists from confusing it with the old bullring, called the *Plaza de Acho,* built by Viceroy Amat in 1765, just across the Rimac River. The Plaza *de Toros* was part stone and part cement, constructed in a big field that was once part of a large hacienda and from which one could see piles of adobe bricks and mounds sticking out of an old Indian burial ground.

We were lucky to get a pair of good seats that gave an unobstructed view of the center of the bullring. Leon saw a couple of acquaintances and nodded. Below us in a box was Pepe Romano and Maria Camargo. Pepe grinned and pointed to the seats. I could read his mind. It telegraphed, "How do you like these seats?" Maria Camargo gave me a big smile and brushed back her hair.

The stirring notes of "La Virgen de la Macarena" reached into the roots of my hair and the pageantry started. Groups of toreros marched out in gorgeous costumes followed by picadores on their well-groomed horses and attendants in colorful array, pearl buttons flashing in the sun, and silver sparkling from the bridles of the horses.

"See those men over there," pointed Leon. "They are the banderilleros. They carry barbed darts fixed up with colored paper flags which they will later throw into the neck of the bull. Sometimes these darts have firecrackers attached to them. They drive the bull crazy with frenzy."

This was drama or anything else you preferred to call it. Leon said it was courage, grace and rhythm pitted against the massive strength of the bull and called it a symphony in danger.

"Don't look now," said Leon, "but there is a very badly matched pair sitting about five rows below us to the right. I didn't know they knew each other so well."

I paused and then got a quick peek out of the corner of my eye. Wearing the same flowered dress she had when I first saw her was Lisa Morel. She was smoking a long cigarette and reading a newspaper. Beside her was Max Martellini and he looked very dapper indeed.

The first torero who returned after the parade was a mulatto named Ruiz. He was the clown of the bullring. The Indian Rubber Man. He had been gored several times but had managed to escape severe injury. The bull was a small one and Ruiz executed movements that were not found in the bullfighter's manual and the crowd roared. He rolled under the bull's belly, pulling its tail and even rode it for a few seconds until he was thrown off. The bull finally got Ruiz between its horns and threw him into the lap of a spectator. A couple of hats greeted this gesture as well as a half-filled bottle of wine which miraculously remained intact and Ruiz drank from it as he passed under the seats back to the dressing rooms.

The next two fights were performed by novices building up their reputations. The bulls were half-grown and the toreros were somewhat stiff and awkward at times, but they weren't bad. They finally killed their bulls and received scattered volleys of clapping and *oles!* But the applause was being reserved for the main event, and the principal figure, *el hombre muy macho,* Dolletta, the idol of the bullring.

Dolletta came out to a thunderous ovation and the air was filled with hats, newspapers and programs. He bowed to the crowd and the roar increased. He was tall and gaunt and his hawk face was tanned and lined by fifteen years in the arena. He walked to the center of the ring, his black felt cap under one arm, his cloak folded and resting on the other, and bowed to the audience again.

The bull, a big black animal with reddish eyes, ran out of a stall, stopped and stood pawing the ground, his jaws dripping with saliva and his tail twitching back and forth like a flicking whip. He rushed at Dolletta, who gracefully eluded the charge. This was repeated for about five minutes, the bull snorting and attempting to grind Dolletta into the dust and the torero melting away from it as if he were treading on air. The bull rushed again and a banderillero stepped from behind the safety of a wooden wall and plunged two barbed spears into the neck of the animal and stepped back to the wall again. It was split-second timing. The now enraged bull stormed at Dolletta, who easily avoided the frenzied rush. Dolletta was fast on his feet and moving methodically. If the serious groin wound he had received in Spain a year before bothered him, it was not apparent. The black monster now stood pawing the dry earth. The air seemed charged with electricity. The foam that dripped from his lips was tinged with pink and the crowd was roaring for the kill. Dolletta obliged them. He held his sword under the folded cloak and as the animal stormed at him, he thrust it through the heart. The applause became deafening and the cries of *ole!* came in the roar of an avalanche as Dolletta bowed and awaited the coming of the horses to drag away the carcass. Dolletta killed two more bulls that afternoon. The last one was the largest and most ferocious and his ears and tail went to an attractive girl who, it was whispered, was Dolletta's current mistress.

Pepe Romano got up from his chair as the roar of the crowd died down. "Hey, pal," he yelled. "Come over to my place in Ancon when you have some time. Bring a friend. Stay as long as you want if you pay the rent."

Maria Camargo didn't think the remark was very funny nor the invitation particularly well timed. She twirled an arm around Pepe and hurried him to a lower exit.

I'd just gotten home and showered when the phone rang. It was Hetty Telger. She certainly moved fast. She wanted to know if I cared to attend a party that evening at the home of a Chinese friend. She said her husband would be with her and they would pick me up at eight o'clock.

The Mong residence was in a section of Orrantia close to the Columbian Embassy. The dinner was tastefully served on tables set up in the garden in back of the house over which banana and fig trees threw a cool curtain of shade. Practically all of the wealthiest members of Lima's Chinese set were there as well as many of the city's well-known residents such as Pepe Romano and Maria Camargo.

There was even an Armenian who spoke several languages, including Norwegian, who worked for one of the airlines. He jokingly told me that he was a former camel drover who lost his job at the opening of the Suez Canal which killed the caravan business, and decided to go modern by accepting a job with the airline. He had in tow an Englishman who was once a commando in North Africa and had a big hole in his left shoulder from a Schmeisser. The Englishman, a jolly fellow named Ronnie Harper, worked for an importing company. Harper mentioned some of the "old days" when he and some buddies pooled their resources and bought a fast boat, doing a "bit of business" from Tangier to Marseilles, principally in American cigarettes.

Real Chinese food, Cantonese style, with a few added embellishments loaded the several tables in the garden. Big heads of green cabbage bristled in porcupine fashion with shrimp and pickles impaled on bamboo splinters. A row of rockfish with frog-like heads and bodies of bass lay steamed whole in sweet egg and mustard sauce covered with slices of pineapple and coconut.

Another specialty was a large bowl containing sliced mushrooms combined with a crunchy edible seaweed and thin wafers of abalone simmered in a soy sauce, which was surrounded by roast suckling pigs, their skins brown and done to a turn, bits of meat imbedded in crisp, crunchy batter, a tureen of chicken soup in which floated toasted almonds, bean sprouts and egg beaten to a light froth. A colorful backdrop completed the scene with fruits of the country overflowing in several baskets; bananas, cherimoyas, the custard apple of the tropics, figs, papayas, pineapple, grapes and mamay.

Pepe Romano was wearing a white suit that was too small for him and tried to cover up the shrinkage by wearing a big flower on his lapel the size of a corsage. I got a good look at Maria Camargo and decided that while her torso was delightful, her legs were on the heavy side, but I understand that Pepe liked sturdy underpinnings and every man to his own taste. She was hovering about Pepe, who was devouring a shrimp and gave me a warm smile.

"Hello, pal," he said reaching for another shrimp. "I knew that I would find you here." He slapped me on the back and laughed. "You are always around when they serve good food. Have a camarone. They are the best."

Hetty Telger came over with a dish of the abalone, seaweed and mushroom combination which I found delicious. I got her a brandy and soda in return, and we sat down on a bench under a clump of banana trees.

"Did you have fun at lunch?" she asked.

"Wonderful," I said. "I could easy have become a permanent house guest, I was so spoiled by all the good food and especially the attention."

Apparently she understood by that more than I had actually meant. She patted me playfully on the cheek. "Let's get another drink. These people will probably think I've done all sorts of things to you hidden away in this corner."

"I don't mind," I said innocently.

This was the beginning of some sort of build-up. She looked around to see if anybody was within hearing distance. "Don't be surprised if someone should visit you one of these lonely evenings."

I was at a loss for words at the moment. I opened my mouth but nothing came out and I must have looked like a shark coming up for air. Real foolish. Hetty ran her fingertips over my hair, picked up her drink and walked over to another corner of the garden where her husband was speaking with a group of guests.

It was around ten that night that Hetty and her husband dropped me off at my apartment. Her remark earlier in the evening still stuck in my mind, and the long, slow look she gave me when we said goodnight couldn't mean anything but that something was definitely going to happen. The only question was when.

But there was no reason to let my mind dwell on it, and after I'd fixed myself a brandy, I sat down with the evening's *Comercio* and turned to the section which contained the *Noticias Policia,* which gave a resume of all the crimes committed during the day as well as an entire streamer of photographs that looked like the graduating class from a reform school.

Leon, I thought, was probably back at Headquarters burning the midnight oil, fitting together the pieces of his biggest puzzle at the moment. The murders of Barkovit and Graciela seemed to mesh in a vague way, but there was one other piece that I couldn't fit in. Lisa Morel. Aranyi had really confused things with his bit of information. And now Martellini attached to Lisa.

A half-hour after I'd gotten home, the phone rang, and a soft, warm voice that wasn't whispering said, "This is Hetty. May I come up?"

I felt like a shark coming up for air again.

"Hello?" Hetty asked.

"I'll meet you at the door," I said, my voice much more hoarse than I liked.

She'd had hardly enough time to go home and come here, and yet she'd managed to change her clothes. I wondered about that but only for a second as I looked at her.

She looked terrific in a sheer, fluffy, black dress and a black hat with a big, wide rim. The dress was cut so low it practically opened to her waist Hetty sat down and folded her hands in her lap very demurely.

I got her a frapped creme de menthe and a straight brandy for myself.

She raised a shoulder, showing the swell of her bosom and I took her hat and put it on a chair. I sat down next to her and deliberately she put her arms around my neck and kissed me hot and long, her mouth open.

"I've been dying to do that ever since I saw you," she murmured. We kissed again and I held her tightly. Hetty was different in the sense that hers was not wild, unabated passion like that of Graciela Salinas. It was carefully measured and burned right down to my finger tips.

It was no secret what Hetty had come for. Almost immediately she was in the bedroom, her dress hanging partially down her sides. She had the most magnificent body I had ever seen. I put my arms around her shoulders and kissed her. The dress slipped even lower. She was sitting on the bed with a hand on a shoe when the. door bell rang!

The visitor turned out to be Victor Brown, a brassy American I'd met at Hetty's at lunch, who worked for a mining company. Apparently he'd been drinking ever since lunch and had run out of drinking partners.

I refused to let him in and told him to go to hell, but the damage had already been done. Hetty came out of the bedroom and picked up her hat from the chair. She was really angry and I didn't blame her. I was seething myself. Hetty fidgeted with her handbag.

"I really must go," she said, but refused to look up at me. But she did put her hand to my arm as I saw her to the door, as much as to say that regardless of how she felt she realized it wasn't my fault. But I knew that as far as she was concerned, my apartment was completely out of the question for further meetings, simply because you never could tell who might be at the door.

CHAPTER FOUR

To my complete astonishment, Hetty came by at nine the next morning with her husband and told me they were going to take me to the auto races. They had made up my mind for me. Hetty acted as though she hadn't even seen me the night before and from her husband's expression I was sure he knew nothing about her visit—at least he didn't know that it was I who was visited.

"We saw your friend Enrique Leon a few minutes ago and he said he'd meet you at the starting point," she said.

Already Lima was practically deserted. Plaza San Martin was quiet. The daily hum and buzz had gone out of the air. The horde of street vendors had left their customary places for better pickings and the only people around was an old couple standing at the stop for the Miraflores bus. The auto races from Lima to Nasca, a warm-up for the big race, the Lima-Trujillo grind which was two months away, was about to begin from the starting point on the Malecon Cisneros, where a big banner advertising a soft drink was stretched across the road. Practically every street vendor in Lima was there, the sellers of pastry, cold drinks, ice cream, sandwiches, peanuts, and fruit. There were even several Indian women who squatted before charcoal fires glowing beneath a clump of willows where various concoctions bubbled in blackened pots.

Somebody tapped me on the shoulder. I turned around and Leon greeted me as if he hadn't seen me for months.

"Why aren't you out solving murders?" I ribbed him.

"Well, this is as good a place to study the crowd as any. The murderer of Barkovit and Graciela Salinas is probably going to watch the race. He might even be one of the drivers."

A couple of hot rods and souped-up coupes of different manufacture sputtered, roared, chattered and rattled as their owners warmed up the motors. Pepe Romano's Ford roared as he stepped up and down on the gas. He was wearing an aviator's cap of World War I vintage and the inevitable yellow scarf, knotted at the throat. Pepe smiled at the passers-by and his co-driver, Jorge Mendez smiled too. After all, they Were in this dramatic thing together.

Romano was confident of victory and publicly said so. Last year he told me he had finished tenth in a field of twenty-five but blamed his poor showing on sabotage. He claimed that a man had been lurking near his garage and that his motor had been tampered with. Leon said one of the tabloids carried the story and played it up to the limit with the result that sales for the edition had soared.

The cars roared away from the finish line in a cloud of dust, and gasoline and oil fumes. Romano waved his yellow scarf and disappeared around a corner. In a matter of ten minutes, we counted 30 cars, starting the race.

"There's nothing to see now," said Leon. "A lot of the people follow the cars and watch from different points along the route. Anyway, we can read all about the race and who won in the evening papers.

We said good-by to Hetty Telger and her husband, who said they were going to a nearby restaurant, and declined the invitation to join them.

Leon had his Anglia on a side street and we headed for Miraflores. A low, dense mist began to creep in from the sea and the jacaranda trees dripped with it making the purple blossoms appear almost black in the damp eddies that swirled through the calles and avenidas.

Around the adobe huts and pock-marked walls of the Miraflores market section, a respectable distance away from the neat and foliage-covered part, the mists were even heavier and the market was completely shrouded in vapors. Even then, it was open for business as usual with trucks being unloaded of baskets of shiny green avocados, stalks of bananas and ears of corn.

On the other side of the market was the flower section and the road ran right by a muddy drainage ditch that ran under the shacks where the flowers were sorted for sale. The water probably kept the flowers fresh and well saturated with a goodly supply of microbes to give the person who sniffed them more than just a whiff of perfume. An urchin was busily making up small bunches of violets while his mother, sisters, aunts and cousins hovered about arranging pots containing geranium, floribundia and heliotrope which filled the damp air with an overpowering scent and formed a second layer under the mist.

The sun tried to break through but it was a sickly effort that soon faded before the mist barrier. The trees continued to drip and the flower vendors rustled their merchandise.

I got a glimpse of a ragged *cholo* beside his moulting burro who pulled a brown wool scarf higher up over his face until only the bridge of his nose and his eyes were exposed. That gesture was a strange one and I questioned Leon. He explained that the earthy inhabitants of Peru have a dread of the winter season with its fevers and sicknesses which they believe creep into their noses and mouths from the mists.

Leon laughed. "He will feel better after he has a big drink of pisco, and then some rolls and cheese and some good hot coffee with boiled milk."

A small crowd loomed out of the mist at the side of the muddy ditch. A lone policeman was vainly trying to keep it away from something and he wasn't doing very well. Leon stopped the car and we got out. The policeman was glad to see us and got a little braver shoving back a couple of youths who tried to elbow their way past him.

A hat lay on the ground and beside it a livid face stared up at us, the tongue protruding and the eyeballs rolled back showing practically all white, the dead-white of the belly of a deep sea fish. The head now matched the carcass which was on the obese side. A piece of cord, knotted at the back of the thick neck, was partially sunken in a mound of bluish folds.

The woman who sold the violets took a good look at the fly covered clod and fervently crossed herself. "Santa Maria!" she gasped. "It is Carlos, the *huacero*." It was Carlos, all right, stiff, cold and dead in the flower section of the market.

"Do you know him?" I asked Leon.

Leon nodded. "Everybody knew him. He sold *huacos,* old ceramics dug from Indian graves, in front of the Hotel Europa. Of course, some of them were fakes, but the tourists didn't know the difference. Once in a while, he would make a trip to the mountains for a fresh supply with his burro. It must be around here someplace." We looked in the scrubby bushes but the burro was nowhere.

"That's strange," said Leon. "That burro was always with him. There is only one answer. He must have been killed some place else."

Some of the market people must have notified the police because a shiny, new Ford squad car pulled up filled with cops carrying sub-machine guns and rifles. They must have thought they were going to a gang war. A sergeant threw a hunk of canvas over the body and told the crowd to go home. In a few minutes, the wagon arrived and Carlos was on his way to the morgue.

"Chalk up another murder for the fellow who did away with Barkovit and Graciela Salinas," said Leon. "I'll stake my reputation on that."

"But a guy like Carlos," I insisted, "what could he possibly have that the murderer wanted?"

ROBERT A. LEVEY

"The same thing that Barkovit and Graciela had. Information. Persons like Carlos Lento move around a lot. They hear and see a great deal. Look at the rope around his neck. I have been around here all my life and I know the people here. They do not kill with a rope. They use the knife. I wager you anything that Carlos Lento was murdered elsewhere and brought here.

"I'm going over to Headquarters and it looks like another late night for me. I'll drop you off in Plaza San Martin if you like."

"That's good enough for me," I said. "I might even see a movie."

"Also I'm going to take a steam bath this afternoon. Join me?"

"Sure. Where?"

"I'll meet you at Headquarters," Leon said, stopping the car and letting me out.

Crossing the Plaza, I ran into the lady dude rancher I'd met at Hetty's coming out of one of those re-conditioning beauty salons on Ocona. Only this time, they didn't do a very good job. Her hair was blacker than ever and orange lipstick made her lips look like two ripe mangoes, the kind of lips whose flavor you wouldn't want to sample. An oleander blossom was stuck over her left ear above a black lariat of a curl and a shawl made up of at least twenty different colors was thrown across her shoulders with the same casualness that a cover is tossed on a pool table at closing time.

She grabbed me by both hands. "For heaven's sakes, where have you been? I've been trying to find you ever since lunch yesterday."

"Just about every place," I said rather truthfully.

"Well, I'm taking a big house on the road to Chaclayo," she said. "You should see it. Big pool. A wonderful view of the mountains. A big bar. Plenty of bedrooms. Why don't you come over tomorrow? I'm moving in this afternoon. Stay a few days, a week, a couple of weeks, I don't care. There's room for everybody." She closed up those bright orange lips and stood looking at me with an expression that said, "Well, what more do you expect me to say?"

"Thanks, Clara," I said. "I can't say definitely tomorrow, but I will be around."

A deal like that from the right party and I would have picked up my toothbrush and extra shirt and packed a bag in fifteen minutes flat, with a shower and shave thrown in for extra measure. But a fellow would have to be awfully lonesome to spend an evening in Clara Bentley's big house in the country. A driving tropical rainstorm, a few shutters beating against the sides of the place and Clara walking down the long corridor would have sent even the most hardy male running into the night

At three o'clock I arrived at Headquarters. All the big boys there had been in a huddle and were convinced the three murders were the work of the same person, and that possibly they were members of some kind of an organization. What kind? That was a good point.

From Headquarters we drove to the Hotel Metro. The steam baths there were the best in Lima, the only ones. A few months previously, Leon related, competition had been removed when a boiler blew up in a rival establishment at the other end of town, permanently parboiling the proprietor, who was also the manager and chief masseur.

Here you paid the man at the desk ten soles. He gave you a key for a locker, the privilege of stewing yourself down to the size of a midget and later taking a plunge in the pool if you had enough strength left to stay afloat You could also get a massage but there was a slight extra charge for that

We got a couple of lockers side by side, undressed, slipped the keys which were held by leather thongs over our wrists, and headed for the steam baths. The first one was warm, the second hotter and the third like the crater of a volcano. A lot of different languages came out of the steam, Spanish, of course, and German, Italian, French, Polish and occasionally English, the American variety. There were even voices several octaves higher than the usual male tone which momentarily made me feel that perhaps it was ladies' day at the Turkish Baths—a whale of an idea.

Leon and I hit the middle room after about fifteen minutes and ran into a group of narwhals with sagging navels drooped over their towels who were talking about the stock market, punctuating their conversation by spitting on the floor and flipping off handfuls of old beer that oozed from their pores. One was even shaving, feeling about his face with a razor and wiping the softened hair off on his towel.

There were a couple of muscular Frenchmen in the last room, which was a real inferno, and we stood it for about ten minutes and returned to the middle room, after which we hit the showers. An old man with a shock of white hair came out of the shower room as we were rubbing the big towels over our backs. He nodded pleasantly and went over to his locker.

"That is Professor Reimer," said Leon. "You ought to see his collection of Chimu ceramics. They demonstrate a greater variety of positions in bed than the French ever invented. The only group as good as his is in the National Archaeological Museum. Interestingly, they never show them to women."

Professor Reimer walked up and bowed slightly. "Good afternoon, gentlemen." He knew Leon and included me in the greeting. "This is a wonderful place. Very good provided you don't overtax your faculties. I come here twice a week and I must say there is nothing like it."

We went upstairs wrapped in big, warm towels where there were dozens of comfortable lounges around the pool. One of the fat men from the steam rooms was already asleep, his loud snores alternating between the sound of ripping canvas and the hollow moan of a distant fog horn. Another blubbery sea lion woke up and snapped his fingers for a waiter. The sounds of *oye! mozo* and a crescendo of hissing that sounded like a nest of rattlers drew the attention of a group of waiters who ran about the room with bottles of various cold drinks to assuage the desperate thirst of the customers. The poor waiters took all kinds of abuse from the reclining hulks as they tried to fill the sudden rush of orders as quickly as they could.

Leon remarked that the sudden surge of activity about the lounges was nothing unusual. The same thing went on daily, and the waiters had the same kind of insults hurled at them by the same persons and apparently had become immune to the tirade. We relaxed for an hour and went downstairs to the locker room. Leon's locker was slightly ajar.

"Strange," he said. "I could have sworn I locked it."

"Anything missing?" I asked.

Leon examined his clothing thoroughly and felt in an inside pocket for something that wasn't there. "Just my little notebook," he said, "but whoever took it didn't get much. I keep all of my important information at Headquarters. Still, it's a good thing I filed my daily report before we came here." He thought a moment. "But this is a good thing. The person who committed the murders is getting worried, and when a murderer is worried he may do something that will give him away."

Leon went back to Headquarters and I walked back to my place which was located in the Edificio Bala, one of the newer apartment buildings in Lima, in time to see a beachwagon pull up at the entrance. The driver, wearing a pair of white coveralls with the name Rimac Airlines sewed on the back with red thread, got out and opened the rear door. Patty Parsons stepped out. She had two big pieces of luggage and one of those flight bags that all airline hostesses carry, a thing with a long carrying strap that resembles a small haversack. I'd met her on the movie location.

"Carry your bags?" I asked. "Kind of low in funds today. Need the price of a cup of coffee."

"Go ahead," she said, "but don't strain yourself. They're pretty heavy." She was right. They were heavy and bulging at the side.

I was going upstairs anyway. Patty lived on the floor above me with another girl I hadn't seen yet.

We got into the elevator and stopped at her fifth floor apartment. The placed smelled musty. She opened the windows and tossed her flight bag on a chair.

Patty stretched her arms and yawned. "You'll have to excuse me for a while. I must get out of these things. The trip seemed so long and it was devilishly hot in Miami."

She went into the bedroom and I looked around the place. There was a couple of magazines from Santiago, one of which was splashed with photos of girls sitting on terraces and others cavorting on the beach at Vina del Mar. They were certainly torrid looking numbers and I wondered if Chilean girls were all they said they were.

You got an idea what kind of girl Patty was by the contents of her bookcase. There were two volumes of Jones's work on Freud next to a book titled *On Love* by Stendhal, two volumes on existentialism by Jean-Paul Sartre and a black-bound copy of an English translation of Baudelaire's *Flowers of Evil*. There was even a small paperbound pamphlet of poems by Patty Parsons from the Prairie Press. I read some of them. Maybe Freud would have understood them. I didn't.

Patty was probably a creature of moods, which is a very distasteful condition with anybody, but particularly distressing in women. She could likely run the gamut from abysmal to zealous in a couple of minutes and then start all over again. I knew she was after some airline pilot, most of whom were tall, good-looking fellows with wavy hair, winning smiles and big bankrolls.

Patty came out of her bedroom well scrubbed. Her hair was pulled back tight in a ponytail and tied with a pink ribbon. She was wearing a pair of black velvet matador pants with laces at the knee and a white blouse. The outfit wasn't for her. She was a little too big in the rear and had heavy calves, and pants don't go very well on persons with that kind of build. But she thought she looked good and I let it go at that.

She poured two drinks from a bottle of prepared Manhattans and threw in some ice cubes.

"*Salud!*" she said and we touched glasses. She was acting extremely cordial, considering I'd met her only once. From the weight of her luggage she must have had something she could turn into ready cash.

Patty opened one of the pieces of luggage which was crammed with women's clothing, shoes, underwear, nylons, handbags and hats.

She handed me a pipe. "I even thought of you," she said.

"Thanks," I said, quite astonished. Patty had a few fleeting moments in her make-up when she thought of others. But they were very few. There was only one person in Patty's life. Patty.

I wasn't going to ask her if she had been offered a screen test after her part as one of the temple maidens in "The City of Emeralds," but I sipped my drink instead. Among the dozens of things crammed into a twenty-two year existence by this mixed-up kid was a dramatic career on the stage, if you could believe her, which I didn't. Anything you mentioned she had done. She was a writer, painter, expert swimmer and photographer. She was an expert liar, too. But she said something that made my ears stand up.

"That man Barkovit who was murdered was a pretty good customer," she said. "Bought a dress and other things after every trip." She shrugged her shoulders. "Lose one customer, get another."

I picked up a cork-colored pair of shoes with high heels and looked them over. "Don't tell me he wore stuff like this."

"Don't be sarcastic," she said. "He told me he was buying everything for a girl named Salinas."

"At least they have one thing in common now," I said.

"What's that?" she asked.

"They're both dead," I said.

ROBERT A. LEVEY

There was no reaction whatsoever.

We had another drink and she began to fumble around with the other piece of luggage. She opened it and began to arrange items of clothing on the sofa. I got the hint.

"You don't mind leaving, do you?" she asked. "I don't want to seem like I'm rushing you out of here, but I have some women coming up here soon and for obvious reasons they prefer to be alone in here."

"Sure," I said. "Guess I'll drop over to the Bar Europa. Some of the boys ought to be there by this time."

She opened the door quickly and her forced smile vanished even before the lock clicked.

But I never got to the Bar Europa. Pepe Romano was standing in front of the Club Excelsior, a big white building fronted with fluted marble columns that showed a distinct Italian influence. He was wiping the back of his neck with a handkerchief showing an initial that was visible ten feet away. The sun was a ball of fire and the temperature must have been over a hundred and the humidity ninety-nine percent.

"You're just in time, pal," he said slapping me on the back with a sticky palm. "It's too hot to be walking around. Bad for the heart. Come in and join me for a cool drink."

Two classes of people are members of the Club, those with a lot of money and members of old families. Romano didn't have much money but his family went all the way back to Pizarro. One of his ancestors was said to have been in the same room with Pizarro when he was murdered and perhaps even went through Francisco's pockets when the founder of Lima hit the floor. Family fortunes have been founded on less.

Romano nodded to the man at the desk. This probably meant that I was his guest. He took me by the arm and led me to the men's room. "Have to freshen up a bit," he said. He ran the cold water and splashed some on his face and hair, then ran a comb through his long, wavy hair. Then he took off his jacket. Big sweat stains ran all the way under his arms to his waist. Romano took a bottle of cologne from a shelf over the sink, squirting the contents under his arms and dabbing at the overflow with a towel. Then he put on his jacket.

"Boy, that is wonderful!" he said. "It's almost as good as a shower."

Romano didn't smell sweaty now. He smelled like cologne, the forty-nine cent variety.

We went into a room that had a bar and a couple of dozen tables surrounded by chairs. Each table had a leather cup and a pair of dice that seemed to be part of the furnishings. The dice were already clicking at some of the tables to determine who would pay for the drinks, and the unlucky guys got hit with some pretty good checks.

Romano picked up the leather cup and dice from the table. "I'll take care of the drinks, pal. I have an account here. But let's shake, anyway. I want to see how good you are."

"Sure," I said. "High or low?"

"High," he said.

Romano rattled the dice in the cup and rolled. He got a six. I came up with a seven.

"That's the way it is with me," he said. "Bad at gambling but a sensation with the women."

We both ordered gin con gin, which is gin with quinine water and a slice of lime. Why it was called that name I never found out but it always tastes good.

"How are things going with you?" asked Romano. "Are you enjoying yourself here?" Pepe took another piece of fried yuca. He had already eaten a dish of the starchy tuber which tasted like potatoes and under other names of mandioca and cassava is made into starch, glue, alcohol and even a rival to prunes as a favorite boarding house dessert.

"Things are interesting enough," I said. "Never a dull moment. But there is somebody around here who doesn't seem to like me. I'd like to know who the hell he is and do something about it. I came here for a vacation and I don't want to go back in worse shape than I was when I started."

I told Romano what happened, and he almost knocked over his glass when he got the news.

"Really! Don't tell me. How is it possible? I didn't think such things could happen these days, but you must be careful. Do you have a permit to carry a gun?"

"No," I said. "That wouldn't be a good idea. It might lead to more trouble. Anyway, I don't think the police like the idea of a foreigner walking around with a gun tucked under his arm."

"Leon could arrange it for you easily," he said. "A word in the right place is all that is needed."

"No," I said. "I'm not going to bother Leon. I'm going to leave things as they are."

Romano shrugged his shoulders. "Suit yourself, pal. But I know what I'd do in your place."

He lifted his glass. "*Salud!* Stay off the street corners at night and stick to the women. Of course, they can kill you, too, especially if you get a real jealous one. It is a good thing that some women are trusting."

"You should know, pal," I said inflating his ego. "They tell me that you know all the women in Lima, I'm not counting the ones in Arequipa or Trujillo."

"A double *salud* to you, pal," said Romano. "You are so understanding."

We went outside. I didn't mention the road race, assuming Pepe would have if he had won. As it was, it would have been a very sore subject; Romano had finished next to last place this time.

Enrique Leon almost collided with me as I rounded the corner of Azangaro after buying a newspaper.

"Well, well," he said. "I was just over to your place to pick you up. You don't have to look at that paper. Get a late edition and get all the news."

"Okay, *amigo*," I said. "Anything new on the murders?" I told him about Patty Parson's ex-customer, Josef Barkovit and Graciela Salinas.

"We know about that," said Leon. "Barkovit was sweet on Graciela, but she was nothing but a gold digger. I wonder if the poor boob ever found out before he was murdered?"

"Found out anything around the Miraflores market?"

Leon puckered up his face. "Not much. At first, there was the possibility that Lento may have been the victim of some of his so-called friends during a drinking bout you never can tell what some of them will do with a load of bad pisco in them. But we had to throw that possibility out of the window. Carlos Lento was too well liked and we couldn't find a single person who would admit to being on bad terms with him. His murder was the work of a clever person, not one of those illiterate vendors from the market section. We have questioned about every person around but you could get the same answers from a burro. Nothing. As for Graciela Salinas, now we are convinced that she made an appointment with a person unknown when she got the phone call the night you saw her. We found lipstick smears and bits of broken finger nails on the bridge railing. Her hands were bruised and her finger nails were ragged. There is no doubt in my mind that she was right on the bridge and thrown into the water."

"What's up?" I asked.

"I've turned guide today," said Leon. "A friend of Director-General Moran's came in yesterday morning and I've been detailed to show him around. You might learn something, too."

The friend, a clergyman from a small town twenty miles south of London, was a tall, spare individual. His name was Hawley Clark and he was interested in altars, carved paneling and churches in general. Especially old ones. We took him to the oldest.

The Reverend Clark shook my hand with such enthusiasm that his glasses slipped off one ear and hung dangling over his face. "Imposing looking place," he said looking at the weathered stones, "a bit like those old spots we have in England without the ivy."

Pizarro is said to have laid the first stone and carried the first beam that went into building the Cathedral on the east side of the Plaza de Armes. Several times destroyed by earthquakes and rebuilt, the present structure was started in 1746, and time had mellowed its stones into soft pinks, yellows and grays.

We mounted the steps and entered the chapel at the right of the main entrance where the remains of Pizarro could be seen in a glass covered casket. The Reverend Clark peered at the bones over his glasses and casually walked by. What seemed to interest him more were the magnificently carved choir stalls and the altar designed in the style that typified the luxury of the Viceregal period.

The Reverend Clark was apparently about to write a book on the subject; he took copious notes in a little black book he pulled out of a pocket frequently. He wrote down enough to take care of at least the first chapter of the book.

After about a half-hour of wandering about with our clerical companion, we were about to call it a day when somebody slapped Leon on the back. "Hola, viejo!" said the man. "What are you doing, cutting into my business?"

Leon laughed. "This is Raul Salazar, the best guide in Lima. If he doesn't know about a place, it does not exist."

Salazar grinned. "I am finishing up now." He ushered a group of tourists towards the entrance. "What I need now is some fresh air. It is very close and dusty in the catacombs."

"The catacombs?" pondered Leon. "Oh, yes, they were recently opened. They date from the early days of Lima. Would you care to see them, gentlemen?"

We headed for a long corridor that ended at a flight of half-crumbled steps. Lanterns had been hung on wooden pegs driven into cracks in the walls and threw just enough light on the steps to keep a person from breaking his neck as the staircase seemed to end in a yawning black pit.

The bottom of the staircase was about seventy-five feet below the surface of the street and ended in a sort of a landing on which there was a table with lighted lanterns. An old man gave each of us a lantern and Leon handed him ten soles. The old man thanked us and told us the catacombs were straight ahead. We didn't need that information. We could smell them, the smell of ages, dust and death.

The catacombs were in a big room carved out of solid rock. On all sides, there were niches, some empty, some sealed, that looked like big safe deposit boxes. Names and dates could be faintly discerned on some of the slabs, some of which were as powdery as chalk and others covered with a fine green mossy mold. The lanterns revealed stacks of piled bones and rows of mummified bodies fully attired that followed the centuries in clothing styles. Many of the mummies were dressed in robes. Others had capes, pantaloons with long stockings and silk shirts with lace at the cuffs. Several were dressed in military uniforms. Among them were probably some prominent generals of the times and political figures of bygone centuries.

"Gad!" exclaimed the Reverend Clark as his lantern illuminated a skull that showed even white teeth, a big hat on which a few plumes of feathers still clung, a long cloak and the fragments of a pair of boots. A second beam from the lantern showed a sword with a piece of dried leather wrapped around a ring near the handle that lay near the toes of the boots. The Reverend Clark lifted the lantern higher for a better look when it suddenly crashed to the floor followed by a muffled groan.

"What was that?" I yelled. "What happened to Reverend Clark?"

Our lanterns gave us the answer. In the yellow glow the Reverend Clark lay face down in a litter composed of a pair of eyeglasses, a smashed lantern, a pool of kerosene, plenty of age-old dust and a little blood. Near his shoulder was a jagged piece of stained limestone, part of a slab used to seal the niches in the walls. There was a nasty gash on the right side of his head and his face was a mass of small cuts from the glass of the lantern.

The Reverend Clark felt the side of his head and coughed painfully from the mixture of dust and kerosene fumes. "I must have fallen," he mumbled. "I remember holding up the lantern and then I must have stumbled and struck my head."

"Not very likely," said Leon. "I was standing next to you all the time. There is nothing around here a person could fall over and there is plenty of room to walk."

We held our lanterns along the grinning rows of bodies and the niches above our heads. The lids from the empty ones were tilted against the walls to keep the passage clear. There seemed to be no conceivable place from where a slab could have fallen.

The Reverend Clark was standing a bit dazed with a crumpled handkerchief held against his head and apologizing for his behavior as we helped him back to the table where we got the lanterns. The old man in charge of the lantern department was asleep. We woke him and asked him if he had seen anybody leaving the place during the past five minutes, but he shook his head. It was a waste of time asking him anything. An army could have filed by him while he snored in the semi-darkness and dust.

Somebody had tried to brain either Leon or myself. Definitely not the Reverend Clark. He just got in the way at the wrong time. The guy who did the job had been hampered by poor lighting effects and bad timing. It was enough to make Clark forget carved paneling and old altars for a long time.

On the way up the steps, there was a dry scurrying sound, the kind of sound made by a leather sole on a smooth stone.

"Probably rats," said Leon.

"Sure, big ones," I said, "wearing shoes and running like hell. That hunk of stone didn't just fall out of nowhere. It was hurled by a pair of hands. A big pair of hands. That slab is heavy.

Leon smiled wryly.

The Reverend Clark was still apologizing for the incident when we reached the street. He was a mess. His eyes blinked in the sun from a face caked with dirt and dried blood. Leon hailed a cab and we drove to Headquarters, going in a side door to the Infirmary. Dr. Lopez, the police surgeon did a good job sewing the Reverend up. Lopez also kept a good bottle of brandy around for such emergencies and poured out some stiff drinks. I could see that the Reverend Clark appreciated fine brandy. He drank his neat. We drove him to his hotel where he picked up another pair of eyeglasses. He apologized again for causing, as he said, all of the unnecessary work for Leon and myself. In fact, he later called Moran at Headquarters and apologized again. He certainly was an apologetic individual. However, I was sorry about what happened to him. I didn't want to see Leon getting hurt, either. But I was glad it wasn't me. A couple of previous goings over were about all I could stand.

CHAPTER FIVE

T HERE WAS A tremendous surf in front of the Palomar Beach Club. The beach was supposed to be the next best spot in the world for surf boarding next to Waikiki and the boys on the planks were out in full force. It was just as much fun watching them cavort on the boards this morning as to be doing it yourself. It was also less dangerous sitting on a cool terrace with a tall one in your hand. Leon managed to get two visitor's membership cards which were good for sixty days, so you could walk right into the club without having to be invited by a member.

The club was already crowded with plenty of others interested in the surf action. Maria Camargo was seated at a table with a pair of binoculars focused on the huge rollers that seem to start miles away before they broke on a small beach at the foot of the terrace. Leon got a pair of glasses from an attendant and handed them to me. I could make out several figures on top of a tall wave, a couple of whom were familiar. They were two of the pool boys, big bronzed fellows whose company was much in demand at beach parties. Another board occupant was a well-known polo player who rode the twisting slab of wood as expertly as he did his polo pony. I finally got to see what Maria Camargo was looking at so intently. A long wave started to roll in and headed for the beach at breakneck speed. Pepe Romano was right on top of the glossy red board, smiling his much advertised trade-mark—the wide grin and the even white teeth the girls found so irresistible. Approaching the beach he lay down on the board and came in on the sand with a tremendous glide. Romano picked up the heavy board and propped it against a wall, then bowed to the people on the terrace. He was received with a flurry of handclapping for which he raised his hands over his head in acknowledgment. Maria Camargo got up from her table and waved her handkerchief at him. Pepe threw her a kiss.

Patty Parsons came in with an Armenian who worked for one of the airlines and took the table next to us. She gave me a curt nod and immediately looked in another direction. The Armenian was far more congenial. He came over to our table and ordered a round of drinks. Frankly, I don't know what he saw in the girl. Maybe she had a better side. If she did, she certainly kept it well hidden for the most part. Well, anyway, they were in the same business. At least they could talk shop.

Pepe Romano came up the back steps wearing a flowered black and white shirt and a pair of white shorts. His hair was still wet. "How did you like that ride, pal?" he asked on the way over to Maria Camargo's table. "Neat, wasn't it? We could show those Hawaiians a thing or two, eh, pal? Like the board? Specially made for me by a friend in the lumber business. Took three weeks to make it up. Special wood, you know. The design is my own. There's nothing around here to match it."

Romano pulled up a chair next to Maria Camargo. She dabbed at his ears with her handkerchief like the mother of a small boy who had neglected to wash them. Pepe took the handkerchief and wiped off some beads of water that clung to his long hair and ordered some drinks. Maria opened her bag and paid for them. A lovely arrangement.

Two more boards landed on the beach and their occupants carried them to a shed. They were the two pool attendants I had seen previously. A few minutes later they came by the terrace and I could see they were not going to spend their siestas alone. They received slight nods from two well-dressed women, who were a bit on the plump side, but still attractive, and obviously bored with their husbands who at the very moment were probably already tossing dice in one of Lima's men's clubs.

Leon and I read the silent invitations that passed from the eyes of the two women to the bronzed beachboys. They spelled 'let's not go back to that surfboard, I don't want you to be tired.' They both smiled and lifted their glasses. The two women got up from their table and left. They hadn't even had a drink. There was no need to remain now. Their business for the morning had been completed.

I put down my glass. "I don't want to seem repetitious, but are there any new developments?"

"We're coming along," said Leon. "We know the murders were committed by a Peruvian and not a foreigner, which narrows down the population as far as suspects are concerned by about fifteen or twenty thousand."

"How do you know that?"

"The places where the murders took place," said Leon. "They seem to have been carefully selected. The first one was on the waterfront at Callao, the second the bridge over the Rimac, and the third in Miraflores, near the market, although it could have happened elsewhere. The murderer has a microscopic knowledge of the city and the customs and habits of the people. Who else but a Peruvian could have sneaked into the dock area at Callao, which has a high fence at the entrance and plenty of guards, without being seen?"

Leon seemed to sense some doubt in my eyes. "I hope we don't have to wait very long to find out that it will be a clever one who knows every alley in this city like the palm of his hand."

Leon then came up with the news that the Lima Police were running a cook-out, a sierra or mountain variety of barbecue, on the grounds of the Bartolo winery and vineyard in Barranco, a few kilometres south of Lima, the proceeds going to the Police Hospital.

"Just think," he said, "all we are getting for thirty-five soles. All the food you can eat, plenty of wine and the free protection of half of Lima's plainclothes force. Nobody would dare pull anything funny here."

"Don't be too sure," I said. "Of course, not right out in the open. They don't have to stab or shoot us. It would be a simple thing to poison the wine."

"That wouldn't be hard," he said. "Some of these wines are so bad the addition of strychnine or arsenic would hardly affect the taste."

The vineyard, the oldest in Peru, dated from 1650. Long rows of grapevines stretched miles into the distance, separated from the ocean by sand dunes. Some of the vines sprouted near crumbling ruins and with gulls lazily gliding over a sea of green leaves, a striking picture was revealed. A huge vine formed a roof of leaves and fruit over a long walk paved with faded red brick. The vine was said to be over two-hundred years old and certainly looked it. The gnarled base was as thick as a tree trunk and the many branches curled their way overhead for about a hundred yards. The hanging grapes were black and tart, good for making claret but a bit sharp on the palate.

From the barbecue pits wafted the pleasant odor of roasting beef and it automatically drew us in the direction of the ditches covered with iron grills and tended by Indians. Pepe Romano had beaten us there. He was munching on a big rib and licking the fingers of his other hand. Romano was wearing the same white suit he'd worn to the Chinese dinner only this time it wasn't so white. There were grease splashes on both lapels.

"Hello, Pepe," I said. "What's with 'The City of Emeralds'?"

Romano wiped his greasy fingers on a towel that hung by a ring on a table and run his tongue around his cheeks several times. Then he belched softly. "Why, didn't you know? It's all wrapped up and shipped off to the States this morning. Should hear from them soon. After it's released, we'll probably have a private showing. We'll let you know about it" He changed the subject. "Try one of these ribs before the crowd gets here." He licked the rib again. *"Deliciosa!"*

We got a platter of ribs and sat down at one of the dozens of big tables that had been set up. Romano opened three bottles of claret after holding them under his arm. "Just the time to drink it. Body temperature." The wine was new, tart and slightly astringent. You couldn't drink too much of the stuff.

The food began to arrive when most of the persons had been seated, a specialty being *sancochado,* served by Indian women in bright costumes, practically a whole meal in itself consisting of beef, chicken, potatoes, corn, yuca, cabbage, carrots and other vegetables served in the broth in which they had been cooked. More roast ribs followed and then came *anticuchos,* beef hearts which had been marinated in a hot sauce, cut into cubes and skewered on bamboo slivers and barbecued over small grills which were placed near each table.

"Try some," said Romano stripping a sliver of several and popping one after another in his mouth.

I tried some. They must have been soaked in liquid fire. It took practically a whole bottle of claret to help extinguish the flames. Both Leon and Romano thought this was very funny. Big joke!

The entertainment started with four horsemen moving in a rhythmic canter to within fifty yards of the tables. They were completely dressed in white, white linen pants, white capes, white silk shirts and white, wide-brimmed straw hats. The horses were all of the same color, a shade of soft, dapple gray and they responded beautifully to their rider's commands, sidestepping, prancing, rearing up on their hind legs, all in perfect unison. The riders executed complicated formations that brought applause from the crowd.

The star of the show, however, was a girl, Carmen Ollaya, who came from one of the small villages that cling to the frosty sides of the Andes, and whose skill was known throughout most of Peru. Carmen wore a long white cloak lined with blue stripes, and a wide-brimmed white felt hat. Her mount was a small horse, almost like a pony, a mountain or criollo breed that had adapted itself to the thin air, cold climate and sparse feed of high altitudes. It was an off-white color with a delicate black muzzle and slender legs that met black hooves. The distant Arab blood was evident in the strong head and heavily muscled, barrel chest and the thick, white mane. Every movement Carmen made was done with finesse.

The horse reared in front of Romano, who lifted a beef rib and waved it at the rider. Carmen looked back and winked.

"See how I do it!" said Romano. "That girl will be crazy about me before this cook-out is over."

"Why don't you get a date?" said Leon. "The stables are in back of the winery. There must be enough hay there to get comfortable."

"What would Maria say?" I asked.

Leon formed his hands into claws. "Scratch, scratch!"

"Maria had to see her agent this afternoon," said Romano. "I certainly miss her."

"Naturally," said Leon. "That is very obvious."

"Don't feel badly," I said. "Have a drink of pisco." I poured some of the white liquid and handed it to Romano.

Pepe downed the drink and immediately ejected a stream into the shrubbery in back of him. "Where did you get this stuff?" he protested. "Did you make it yourself?"

"What's the matter," I said. "It's no worse than that exclusive brand your company carries."

Romano put up a protesting hand. "Please. Don't say that. My company carries the finest pisco in Peru. It compares with French cognac. It is the only vintage pisco in the country and has been specially selected for export. Please don't say such things."

Leon was turning purple with laughter and covered his face with a napkin. Romano sipped a glass of red wine and remained silent for a moment. Leon opened another bottle of pisco. "Here, Pepe, try another drink. The last bottle may have been a bad one."

"Nothing doing," said Romano.

Around two, Leon said that he had to get back to town so, we left Romano over still another plate of barbecued ribs and headed back to Lima. The telephone was clanging wildly when I opened the apartment door. It was Clara Bentley. "You ought to be ashamed of yourself," she said. "Here I've been in my nice big house for a whole day and still you haven't shown up. Everybody's been here but you. What are you getting, exclusive?"

"Sorry," I said, "I was waiting for the sun to appear so I could use that pool you were telling me about."

"The sun!" she snorted. "I have news for you, boy. There's plenty of sun here all day. Don't you know that my place is located in the sun belt?"

Clara was catching on fast for a tourist. I didn't know she was aware of the phenomenon that hits Lima during the winter months. The strange thing is that while a blanket of fog frequently hovers about the city making the days bleak, gray and damp, the areas just a few kilometres outside the city limits enjoy plentiful sunshine. I guess Clara had me there. The excuse was rather lame. It looked like I'd have to come face to face with Clara's wrinkles and coal black hair again.

"Can I drop over now?" I asked.

"Of course, you foolish boy," she said. "Come anytime. I'll be expecting you."

I called up Victor Brown, who had a little red British MG, and told him I wanted some transportation. I told him I didn't want to borrow the car. He could come along, too. It was the least he could do after trying to barge into my apartment and spoiling my evening with Hetty Telger. I thought the whole thing was a tremendous idea. I could get revenge on Victor by shoving him off on Clara Bentley, and I began to rub my hands and congratulate myself on the cleverness of the plan.

Victor said he would be glad to come along. He was always drinking and when I told him that Clara's place was well stocked with liquor, he fell for the bait. And as for Clara, she was a big surprise. Victor was so overcome with curiosity that he appeared at the apartment in about fifteen minutes flat.

Clara's place was east of Lima off the Central Highway that eventually snakes itself over the Andes at around 15,000 feet. The house was on a side road a couple of kilometres from the small village of Chaclacayo, and we drove past rows of eucalyptus trees that reminded me of the Santa Anita racetrack. Clara had rented the spot from an Italian doctor who had taken his wife on a six months' tour of Europe. The house was a big whitewashed stucco outfit with wrought-iron grillwork on the windows and balconies all over the place. There were lots of evergreens and flowers and the circular driveway leading to the front door looked like a copy of one in front of a gambling house on the outskirts of Las Vegas on the way to Boulder City.

You should have been Victor's face when he met Clara Bentley and the expression of alarm when she grabbed him by the arm and hustled him towards the garden. I was completely forgotten for the moment which was a very happy one. Victor Brown wore glasses, but he was a little taller and slightly heavier than myself and probably more presentable to feminine eyes, especially big, baggy eyes under a thatch of dyed hair.

The garden had a pool which was nicely shaded by willow trees. A lawn ran like a smooth green fairway on a golf course and seemed to disappear into the mountains in the distance. Patty Parsons was standing in the pool, the shallow end. The Armenian who had brought her along was snoring in a beach chair with a towel filled with melting ice cubes plastered around his head. He woke up and groaned, "I'm dying! Why do I have to drink that pisco? I'm burning up. That last drink tasted like lighter fluid."

"Die, you idiot!" said Patty Parsons. "I told that slob not to drink that stuff and he just goes ahead and slops it like water. Why doesn't he drink scotch like a gentleman?"

I tried to be sympathetic. "Is there a stomach pump in the house? A little workover and he'll be as good as new."

The Armenian groaned even louder and I stepped aside. I didn't want to get hit with any used pisco.

"Throw him in the pool," suggested someone, "That ought to sober him up."

"You might drown him," I said. "Let's take him upstairs."

It took four of us to carry the pisco-saturated Armenian upstairs to a bedroom where we slid him into a bed. The Armenian rolled over and almost hit me with a wild swing. "Save me!" he groaned, "I'm dying." Then he lurched out of the bed and ran into the bathroom. He made it.

Hetty Telger came out of one of the half-dozen doors leading to the garden. She stretched out her hands. "Hello, stranger! I never thought you'd ever come out here at all. Would you have come here if you knew that I'd be here?"

"What do you think?" I said. "Do you think I came here to sample Clara's cooking? I hear it is rotten."

"Shh!" she said. "Do you want Clara to hear you?"

"I don't think she'll hear anything. She vanished with Victor Brown about fifteen minutes ago."

"This is a big house," she said. "Why, it must have all of twenty-five rooms."

"Just the place for a nice party."

"Would you like that?"

"Sure," I said. "It's a lot better than swimming in a pool filled with lukewarm water and then being eaten up by mosquitoes later. That's not my idea of a good time."

"You certainly are a wolf," she said, "but I'll have to agree with you. The pool doesn't look very inviting."

"Is your husband with you?" I asked.

"He's someplace around," she said. "Probably talking about coal mining machinery with a disinterested audience."

I told Hetty why I had invited Victor Brown along and mentioned the night he had ruined our little meeting. Her eyes flashed sparks. "Serves him right. A tour with Clara ought to turn his hair white."

It wasn't long before Victor Brown lurched out of a doorway that led from somewhere and flopped on a chair near the pool. His face was smeared with lipstick, the glaring, orange variety. His hair was a snarled mass and his shirt hung over his pants. There was a strong smell of brandy on his breath.

He twisted his face to a side and glared up at me. "Why, you, you double crosser, you con man, bringing me to a place like this! Why didn't you tell me you only wanted my car? That dame Clara must be crazy. She locked the door and I had to go through the window. You're nothing but a swindler!"

Victor slumped into his chair and blew a cloud of brandy vapors in my face.

"Where's Clara?" I asked. "Did you murder her and steal her brandy?"

"How do I know?" he said. "The last time I saw her she was drinking brandy. She drank more than I did. About a whole bottle."

"That brandy must be reserved for special occasions," I said. "I haven't seen a drop of it around since I came in. You must rate."

"Oh, sure!" said Victor. "She tried to get me drunk in about five minutes and then tried to throw me on the bed. She's as strong as an ox."

"What do you want for nothing?" I said.

I thought Victor was going to brain me with a tray of drinks. "Come on, Victor," I said. "Put on a pair of trunks and get into the pool. The water is a comfortable eighty degrees."

"You fake, you swindler!" he said glaring with a pair of bloodshot eyes.

I went inside. "Hola, pal," said Pepe Romano. For a guy who was supposed to be in business, he certainly worked hard at playing. He was leaning against the bar with a toothpick in one corner of his mouth and a cigarette in the other. The rank, strong odor of the black tobacco swept across my face and made my nose quiver.

"Just had a snack," he said, dislodging the cigarette and toothpick with the same movement. "Have to keep eating in this climate. Doctors say the food here does not have enough vitamins so you have to eat a lot to stay healthy."

"My God, you're eating again," I said belatedly.

"Well," said Romano, "I'm not staying here very much longer. Nothing to do. I'm so lonesome for Maria. Going over to the Aero Club soon. Want to join me? A friend of mine just flew in from the jungle and will be there. Both of us were on a jungle outpost near the Ecuadorian border when we were in the army. It was a miserable place. Always raining. We would have gone crazy if we weren't able to go out for hunting trips once in a while. But you couldn't go very far. Those Indians. Every time I saw a bush move I could feel one of them watching me.

"Perhaps you know my friend," he added. "Jose Figueroa. He studied at UCLA, your school."

"Not my school," I said. "Everybody here thinks that all Americans went to UCLA. Of course, there are other schools like Southern Cal, Cal Tech and the University of California. All good schools but I never made any of them."

"Well, what's the difference," said Romano. "Take the University of San Felipe here. The place is full of fleas. They go with the tuition fees. They turn out good students there, like myself, because you have to be good to concentrate on your studies and fight the fleas at the same time. Want to see my scars?"

"Not today," I said.

Romano went to a closet to get his jacket. I was still standing at the bar which faced an open door leading to the garden.
Hetty Telger stood there for a moment. "Be seeing you," she
whispered.

The portal of the Club Aero is quite *a* place. It is a vantage
point for the gay blades of Lima, most of them members of the
club, where they can stand and appraise the physical charms of
the women on their way to dinner or about to attend a session at
the movies.

A feminine tourist would be rather shocked at the remarks
passed by these doorway gallants if her bodily contours encour-
aged any interest. Such remarks as *"Que linda"* and *"Que her-
mosa"* are common expressions.

But there are others that are not listed in the guide books.
These are *piropos* that take in more of the feminine anatomy than
a pair of nice legs, good breasts or a pretty face. Acknowledgments
of the *piropo* are rarely encountered from the women with the
possible exception of a knowing smile as they walk along pre-
tending to hear nothing.

Luis Hurtado, whose father was the proprietor of a curio
shop near the club and who was a member, was a fixture at the
club entrance. You could set your watch with Luis. Punctually
at seven you could find him standing in the doorway and his
remarks to the passing girls were real gems. To a girl who was
unusually curvaceous in a green, sheer dress he said, "Sweetheart,
if you look so lovely in green, how will you appear when you are
ripe?" And to another, "Oh, what legs! If we were together for just
one night, what wrestling holds we could practice!" Luis pointed
to an attractive girl across the street. "She is the mistress of the
publisher of the newspaper *El Diario*." Another was the daughter
of an army general and the mistress of another member of the
armed force. A smartly dressed matron was the proprietress of
a call house. Luis knew them all. He showed me a small pearl
handled .25 automatic he carried in his pocket.

"A woman's husband once shot at me from a window and I fired back. Got to protect myself, you know."

Romano had disappeared down the long hallway. I didn't feel like meeting his friend and listening to the tales of jungle nights and the Indians. I left Luis standing in the doorway. He'd be there again the next evening.

Max Martellini saw me from across the street and ran over to see me almost getting hit by a cab in the attempt. He shook my hand warmly. "My dear friend, where have you been? I surely thought you would drop by again and pay me a visit. Just a friendly little meeting to take a little brandy with me."

"Thanks," I said. "I know your place is only a few blocks from here, but you know how things come up. There's been a lot of excitement around here lately, murders and more murders."

"How true," said Martellini. "I have been here a long time and one never knows what he may encounter when he arises in the morning. Lima is a most unusual city."

"And the people, too," I said.

"Yes, the people. They are quite different from those found in almost any large city in the world. This is a big place but it is next to impossible to keep anything in privacy."

When I met Leon later, I expressed my suspicion that Martellini may have been shadowing me.

"I wouldn't be surprised," said Leon. "Max has been jumpy lately. I've been watching him closely and Lisa Morel, too. They have been together several times." He folded the newspaper. "There's something funny going on in Max's shop. Lisa has been in and out of it about a dozen times the last two days and I can't possibly imagine her stirring out of her house unless there is something worthwhile in the balance." Leon put the newspaper in his pocket. "I've been closer to them than a flea on a dog. I just hope they haven't seen me."

I must have looked jumpy too, and Leon stared at me. "Say, friend, you need a little diversion. You're getting pale. I think maybe you are taking the investigation more seriously than I am."

"Can't help it," I said. "I'm right in the middle of the thing."

"Why don't you do some writing?" he suggested. "Not about this case, of course. Pedro Vargas, the editor of *El Diaro*, will publish anything you write. Remember the article you wanted to write about the Peruvian vineyards? Peruvians like to have stories written about their country by foreigners, especially of this kind. It will be a good job for you being a student of the grape, wines and brandy for a long time.

CHAPTER SIX

GOT TO work first thing next morning. The National Library and the collection at the university were likely spots for information since they had a number of volumes bound in sheepskin that dated from the 1500's. But since most of the big wineries and vineyards maintained offices in Lima, I looked into the classified section of the phone book under '*Vinos*.' I picked out the address of the Buenaventura Winery, for the first stop, which was listed at 168 Santa Clara, a narrow alley that ran off the Plaza de Armes near the Cathedral.

It took a good fifteen minutes to locate the place which was just across the street from a house said to have been built by a side kick of Francisco Pizarro, squeezed in between a crumbling adobe wall and a residence dating from the time of Viceroy Toledo. The bronze plate on the wall said that. I still had to find the office and located a rickety elevator at the end of a dark corridor that responded weakly to a button, and I had to stop off at every floor and peek out since there was nothing on any door to indicate what was inside. On the fifth floor, I hit pay dirt There wasn't any name there, either, but a large photo of a winery and hacienda that hung on the wall facing the elevator gave me a clue.

There were desks in the office piled with newspapers, magazines, pamphlets, wine labels and an accumulation of dust. A good-looking girl with nice legs, ash-blonde hair, gray eyes and a crystal-clear complexion came out of an inner office. Her figure rippled when she walked. I couldn't tear my eyes away from her for a good solid minute. She wore a charcoal cotton skirt with designs in white at the bottom made by the Paracas weavers hundreds of years ago, and a white turtle neck sweater that showed up just about everything. I could see the soft climate of the Basque country of Spain in her light hair and soft gray eyes.

"How do you do," she said with a hardly distinguishable accent, "can I help you with something?"

I told her what I had in mind and she ran her even white teeth over her lower lip and frowned a little. I liked that.

"I don't know where my brother, Eduardo, keeps such things," she said. "I come here so rarely. You can see what a terrible mess this place is in. But I will look and hope that something of value will turn up."

She reached through the lower stratum on one of the desks and pulled out a magazine with yellowed pages. "*Que suerte!*" she said. "This one has an article written by my grandfather almost forty years ago."

The article was a good one and contained a lot of early history on the vineyards—just what I was looking for—and about court intrigues involving land seizures and colorful personalities associated with the making of wines and brandies. However, I still needed photos or illustrations of some kind.

A stocky, dark character with plastered-down black hair came into the office as I mentioned the photos. He peered over his glasses at me, then removed them and wiped them on a handkerchief and replaced them in his pocket.

"My brother, Eduardo," she said.

Eduardo gave me a hand that was as limp as a damp towel, took his other limp hand and rummaged through a drawer where he said he was positive there were several negatives of just the scenes I wanted. Of course, there was nothing there.

He put up a limp hand. "Never mind. We will find something." He glanced around the room and selected five photographs, taking them, frames and all, off the wall

He handed them to me. "You can have copies made from these when you have the time. They do not have to be returned in any hurry. They only gather dust here."

I put the pile of frames aside as Eduardo handed me a pamphlet of descriptions of the local wines produced.

"I assume you like wines," he said, "or perhaps you would not have come here." He opened a cabinet and took out a bottle of red wine. "Try this. It is vintage 1943, so good that my friends think it was imported from the Bordeaux country of France. Look at the bottle. Even the glass is of a special kind."

The girl's eyes lingered on me a long time. She shook my hand with a small, firm grasp. "I am Elena Remasso," she said. "If there is anything else you may need, please call on us again. Do you have a telephone number in case I have something for you?" I gave her my number and she wrote it down in a notebook she took from her handbag. I was sure that wasn't going to be lost under a layer of dust.

I took the bottle of wine and the framed photographs and thanked Elena and Eduardo. She even walked to the elevator with me which was very nice. I got into the old lift and it sank slowly to the street.

The clouds were hanging gray and damp outside and the phone was ringing when I got back. Elena Remasso was on the other end of the wire and she said that her brother wanted to see me again. By the tone of her voice I gathered that it was she who wanted to see me again and not Eduardo. She said that her brother liked persons who were interested in wine lore and wanted to apologize for not spending more time with me at the office.

Then Eduardo got on the line and told me that he had an unusual collection of antique arms he wanted to show me in addition to a good wine cellar, and when he heard that weapon collecting was a favorite hobby of mine, he wouldn't take no for an answer.

"You must positively spend some time with us at the hacienda," he said. "Even if it is only a few hours."

"Thanks," I said. "You make it too attractive to pass up."

"*Bueno*," said Eduardo. We will pick you up in an hour then.

Elena's Ford beachwagon was in front of the apartment promptly at eleven complete with chauffeur and Eduardo, who sat in the front seat with him.

Elena got out and smiled. "Prepare yourself for a good lunch, Roberto. We have the best cook in Peru." She put her fingers to her lips. "*Magnifico.*"

I bowed. "Thank you very much. You can't imagine how much I appreciate this. I'm sure that you looked at my emaciated body and felt sorry for me."

We got into the car. Eduardo smiled and gave me a handshake with a much better consistency than the previous ones in his office. We turned south on the Pan-American Highway, which sliced through yellow desert sands and in spots through big sand dunes. Spiralling buzzards furnished an overhead funereal cortege for the crosses at the side of the road which marked the places where persons had been killed in bus and auto accidents. Eduardo evidently did not relish the idea of adding other crosses and told the driver to slow down to an even fifty. I was glad he did. I was getting jumpy from the swaying buses moving up on the other side of the road.

The Hacienda Buenaventura in the heart of Peru's grape producing region was a picturesque spot. It was hundreds of years old and had a long history that was made by Jesuits, conquistadors and beautiful women. It had been in the Remasso family for six generations and was the kind of a place that one sees in the movies in a picture of old California with Leo Carillo riding up to the front gate mounted on a palomino.

The Remasso's cook was an Italian who knew his business. He did a magnificent job with a huge platter of *lasagna*, which he brought up hot and steaming to the patio, placing it on a polished cedar table, only to return quickly with a big bowl, the size of a tub, containing squid stuffed with a mixture of toasted bread crumbs and chopped ham, olive oil, Parmesan cheese, black olives, oregano and small sweet peppers, floating in a hot, spicy sauce. This was followed by a ham, smoky and black that had been hanging from the rafters of the storehouse for several years. Crusty loaves of bread came next with plates of ripe olives, sliced turkey and red and white wines. A jellied dessert called *mazamorra morada* made from purple corn, fruits and spices arrived with brandy and cigars.

It was very difficult to get up from the table. Eduardo took me by the arm and led me to a big room with beamed ceilings and a lot of glass cases where he kept his prize collections of firearms and edged weapons. He unlocked a second door and I feasted my eyes on the suits of armor and the swords that hung from the beams.

Eduardo beamed with obvious pleasure when I correctly identified the maker and date of manufacture of a pair of dueling pistols that lay side by side in a velvet lined cherrywood case. He was even more impressed with my smattering of knowledge when I guessed that some of the rapiers that studded the beams in the ceiling came from Toledo.

"We are going to the distillery and later to the wine cellar," he shot over his shoulder to Elena who was close behind us all the time. "We will be back in a half hour or so."

"Don't drink too much in the wine cellar," said Elena. She obviously knew her brother a lot better than I did, which was as it should be.

The distillery was constructed of adobe blocks covered with gypsum and then whitewashed. The date 1690 was burned in a mahogany beam over the doorway. There was no doubt the place was a distillery. A sour vinegary smell lingered and permeated everything and the odor of crushed grapes was in the air. A row of clay jugs lined the wall. Eduardo explained that they were used to transport wine and brandy centuries ago. Bottles and glass were too expensive and scarce in those days. There were charcoal fires glowing under copper stills. Coils spiralled over the tanks and ran into vats filled with running cold water and then out again into an enormous glass jar into which ran a colorless liquid.

Eduardo dipped a finger into liquid and tasted it. "That is pisco," he said, "made from grapes. Carefully made and aged, there is no finer drink on earth."

He showed me two old stills made from copper. They were no longer in use. The date on the bottom of one showed 1690. The other was made by a Carlos Encondero in Madrid in 1730.

"Enough of this," said Eduardo. "Let me show you the wine cellar."

We went back to the house and through a passageway that ran along the edge of the garden lined with fig trees. Eduardo opened a door and produced a lantern and I followed him down a flight of stairs that was so long it reminded one of those descending into the catacombs under the Cathedral. The smell of age was in the air. Eduardo hung the lantern on an iron hook that protruded from the gray walls. It illuminated row upon row of racked bottles covered with dust and cobwebs and large oak barrels that were stacked one above the other almost to the top of the vaulted ceiling.

"Modestly speaking," said Eduardo, "this is the finest collection in Peru and perhaps even in South America. This is the kind of stock one never sees in a store. It is too precious."

Eduardo examined several barrels, turned the wooden faucet on one and filled the two glasses he took from a chest on the floor. The aroma hit the ceiling and bounced back at my nostrils. I sniffed my glass and took a small sip, rolling the brandy around on the tip of my tongue. Eduardo watched me intently.

"Magnificent!" I exclaimed.

"Ah!" said Eduardo. "I knew you would say that. It only confirms my contention from the first time we met that you were an expert judge of fine liquors. Of course, you tried the bottle of wine I gave you."

"It was as good as any Bordeaux red wine," I said. "As a matter of fact, I would compare it with a good Margaux, or perhaps, a St. Julien."

"Thank you," said Eduardo.

The wine was not that good. However, it wasn't bad. I wanted to be nice. I wanted the brandy to keep on flowing. "You know," I said, "with brandy like this I could spend a couple of days right here. I once spent a night in a wine cellar in Germany. I still don't know how I got out of the place."

Eduardo gave me a brandy smile. "Isn't this glorious. It is like liquid sunshine."

I had a couple of more and Eduardo matched me. I felt like going on. The brandy clouds in the close cellar were beginning to make me float. I remembered about Elena upstairs and mentioned her remark to Eduardo, whose mind was slowly becoming a blank.

We got back on ground level and the fresh air hit me right in the face. Elena was waiting. She seemed peeved and I couldn't blame her. We had been in the wine cellar for at least an hour. Eduardo disappeared.

"He's gone to bed," said Elena. "He does that after a few too many. Can't we go someplace?"

"Sure," I said. "How about Ancon. Pepe Romano invited me. We can make his place in an hour or so."

Ancon was a fishing village from pre-Inca times and looked like it hadn't changed a bit since then except for the minor additions of a casino and a couple of white apartment buildings that snuggled up against the side of a cliff.

Romano's uncle owned one of the white apartment buildings, I was told, and I imagine Pepe got away without paying any rent since he was the apple of the uncle's eye, the old boy having been somewhat of a roue himself.

We puffed up the eight floors to Pepe's apartment, which had to be on the very top of the building. Pepe opened the door. "Hi, pal," he said. "Elena, my little dove!" Apparently I could meet no one in Lima whom Pepe didn't know.

Romano's uncle was sitting in a cool-looking wicker chair reading a newspaper. He seemed a first edition of Pepe Romano. His hair was gray and thin in spots but there was a definite sharpness to a face that defied the inroads of advancing old age. His face was deeply tanned, and he was very debonair in a blue sports shirt with white polka dots, a pair of cream-colored slacks and gray sandals. He took off a pair of tortoise shell glasses and shook my hand cordially and nodded to Elena. "I was just about to leave," he said. "Nothing in the newspapers today. Anyway, I have an appointment at the Casino with a friend." He bowed and left the room.

The place was decorated in good taste with bamboo and wicker furniture, bright cotton print drapes, roughly woven scatter rugs and an artistic array of carved women's heads in polished ebony, teak and sandalwood on the walls. It showed a woman's touch: Maria Camargo's.

While we sipped our drinks, the door suddenly flew open and Maria Camargo came in and collapsed in a chair. "For heaven's sakes, Pepe!" she gasped. "Why don't you get an elevator in this place? Every time I come here I feel a heart attack coming on."

"Now, now, *amorcita,*" soothed Romano. "I'll get you a nice cold drink and you will feel better." Pepe retreated to the kitchen and then stuck his head around the corner of the room. "Did you say something, dear?" Maria reached down and took a sandal and threw it at him. "That's for you, you buzzard."

By the time we'd finished our first drinks, the doorbell rang and Romano let in Ronnie Harper and his blonde divorcee friend. "I say, old fellow," he said between trying to catch his breath. "Really, you should have a lift here."

"What do you want?" asked Romano. "A lot of people pay good money to take off weight and here you get the chance free."

"Oh, behave yourself, Pepe," said Maria Camargo. "Why don't you stop talking and get some more drinks? I'm practically dying of thirst."

Romano brought another tray of drinks from the kitchen and we helped ourselves. "I don't suppose that any of you people will believe me when I tell you that my uncle is putting in an elevator next year. He told me that his age really shows up when he climbs the stairs."

"Where are you going to put it?" I asked. "Blast a hole and stick it in someplace?"

"Not inside the building," said Romano. "Outside."

Everybody looked at Romano with amazement but he stood his ground. "The elevator will run in back of the building. That's rather a clever idea, I think."

Unique was a better word. That meant when we went to visit Romano, we got off at the eighth floor patio and walked through Pepe's bedroom and kitchen to reach the living room. It was the sort of thing dreamed up by an architect who hit the bottle once too often.

"Let's go to the Casino for a swim," suggested Maria Camargo. "This place is not Acapulco but it will have to do for the moment."

"Bah!" said Romano. "I can bring along a dozen girls wearing Bikini suits, carrying baskets of mangoes, bananas, pineapples and oranges—and what do you have? The same thing."

"You've forgotten one important thing, darling," said Maria Camargo. "The women may look the same, but will they be so completely *ardiente*? Do you follow me, darling?"

Romano grinned from ear to ear. "You are absolutely right, *querida*. If all women were like you, this place would be the biggest tourist center in the world."

Pepe's uncle was on the terrace of the Casino and he was smoking a long cigar and a good one. The breeze from the ocean wafted the mellow aroma of an expensive Havana that made me hungry for one. Pepe's uncle apparently liked the finer things in life and indulged in them freely. He could. He had the money, but on the other hand there are people loaded with cash who deprive themselves of the enjoyment of a good meal, a fine cigar and a vacation in a decent place.

The beach was cleared of the fishermen, their nets and the stray corvina by this time and the boats were pulled up against a small seawall to await the morning tide. Naturally it was the first time I had seen Elena in a bathing suit, but I certainly was not disappointed. In fact, her figure was much better than Maria Canargo's, Maria being a lusty, taller big-boned damsel. Both were big improvements over Ronnie Harper's blonde friend who was pretty but inclined to being a bit flabby. Probably too much pastry at tea time.

There was a raft a hundred yards off the beach and we all headed for it. We took it easy but I was the first one there. It was already occupied by Victor Brown and a German *fraulein*. We got on the other end and the sudden shifting of weight almost tipped Victor and the girl into the water. The girl laughed but Victor gave me one of the dirtiest looks I've ever encountered, yesterday's notwithstanding.

"Let's go," said Victor to the *fraulein*. Victor probably had a room on the beach in one of those old boarding houses built around 1850. Besides, the raft was hardly the place for what he had in mind. The girl dived into the water. Victor gave me another dirty look and followed her.

"Nice people," said Romano. "Do you know them?"

"I know that fellow. Didn't you meet him yesterday?" I said. "Nice boy, but he had a horrible experience that completely unnerved him. I don't know the girl, but I'd like to meet her." I winked at Elena and she smiled.

"You and your *frauleins*," said Romano. "Didn't you have enough of them during the war?"

"Correction," I said. "There is a big difference. They were Austrian mountain girls with long blonde hair and blouses that almost fell off their shoulders. All we did was take walks and pick edelweiss. What marvelous scenery in the Austrian Tyrol."

"Well, well, well," said the girls in one tone. "Now wasn't that nice?"

I changed the subject quickly. I didn't like the way Elena was looking at me. "Let's go to the Casino and get something to eat."

"I thought we were going there in the first place," said Romano, "Who started us out to the raft?"

Everybody shrugged. "The water looked good," said Ronnie Harper, "but I could do with a bit of a bite now." It was getting late.

"That's a good idea," said his blonde friend. It was almost the first thing she had said all afternoon.

We made for the shore floating and paddling all the way. The terrace on the Casino was crowded but we could still see Romano's uncle. We showered and changed into our clothes. It was starting to get dark. Ancon at night was a pretty place, a miniature Rio de Janeiro, if you have a good imagination. Elena hooked her arm into mine and we headed for the terrace overlooking the sparkling bay.

There was a man standing in the doorway of the Bala building when we got out of Elena's beachwagon. He was wearing a brown suit, a blue sleeveless sweater and black shoes and he watched us, taking quick peeks over the top of a *Comercio*. Maybe he wasn't interested in the financial section of the newspaper because it was upside down but he soon corrected the position and apparently settled down to some serious reading. This was a hard task since the light from the street lamp wasn't very good.

Then he changed his mind and tucked the paper under his arm and lit a cigarette which apparently was not made from vintage tobacco as the rank smoke flowed right by my nose and made me sneeze.

Elena saw me giving the doorway guardian the eye and I wonder what she was thinking about.

"He looks like a plainclothesman to me," I said, "but I may be wrong." They all seem to wear brown suits and sleeveless sweaters. It must be standard equipment with them."

"You must be important," she said. "Are you?"

"Not very," I said. "I don't have the charm of that playboy from the Dominican Republic or the collection of comic books found in King Farouk's bedroom. But there's been a lot of rough happenings going on here lately."

"What do you mean?" she asked.

"Didn't you hear about the time my neck was almost broken in Plaza San Martin? All I was doing was sitting on a bench minding my own business. And still another time in the Barrio Rimac when all I wanted was a package of razor blades and a tube of shaving cream and what happens? I almost get kicked to death. I tell you I'll have to change my name and grow a beard."

"You certainly have led a hard life here," she said, "but I always thought the cab drivers were the only ones who tried to kill anybody."

"Could be," I said. "But right now, I don't think even Lloyds of London would insure me. I'm too much of a risk."

Just then a diminutive streetcar rattled and groaned around the corner of Calle Cueva bobbing up and down with the added weight of the hordes of gamins who hung on the back. The bird in the brown suit and blue sweater folded his newspaper and put it in his pocket and boarded the antique which had a sign marked Brena. He looked back at us and even smiled. Right there I got it! He had been sent by Director-General Moran to keep an eye on me and see that I stayed healthy when Leon wasn't around.

"The police are keeping an eye on me," I said. "They don't want anybody banging me up again."

"I can see the point," she said. "It would be very bad for the tourist business if you returned home with an arm in a sling and a bandaged head."

CHAPTER SEVEN

MARIA CAMARGO WAS giving an afternoon party for Pepe Romano and called me to make sure I would attend. "Pepe likes you," she said. "He always talks about you and when I tell him not to eat so much to keep from getting fat, he tells me that you eat twice as much as he does and still you are slim. That makes him feel better."

"Pepe is always good for a laugh," I said. "If you want the truth of the matter, I haven't eaten in three days what I saw him eat two days ago."

Maria laughed. "And I had to miss it all! Well, no matter what Pepe says about you, I still like you. Be sure to be at El Lago at three."

El Lago was a rustic retreat in the middle of a small lake half hidden by trees and hedges, a favorite spot for intimate gatherings since a small footbridge leading to the entrance could be blocked off making the place a nice, cosy island.

Maria Camargo had the cash so the atmosphere lacked nothing and presented a very festive appearance. A major domo dressed in a white coat and dark pants and wearing white gloves stood at the gate on the footbridge with a list of the guests. It would have been a tough job to crash that party unless you swam over or you were bigger than the major domo, who was an enormous fellow with shoulders that reached over the sides of the bridge.

Hetty Telger was ahead of us on the bridge with her husband. The sun drew sparkling lights from her gown and accentuated the curve of her bosom. I finally got through the customs with Elena and made the interior of the building, which was a replica of a German hunting lodge, with beams in the ceiling, dark paneling and chandeliers constructed of deer horns. The place was already half-filled. Ronnie Harper and his round-faced blonde were sipping drinks at a corner table. Hetty Telger and her husband were seated and chatting with other guests. Even Patty Parsons and the Armenian had managed to make the party.

The Armenian held up a glass and grinned. "Scotch and soda. No pisco today." Patty Parsons gave him a glance that said "And that's all you will drink, too."

A mambo band began to beat out its catchy rhythm and the air was soon filled with 'ooh, ooh, ooh,' the kind of sound that invariably follows the completion of a big meal, sort of a hybrid cross between a belch and a groan, and it was amusing to hear big business executives sound like carnivores at mealtime. But even a few drinks will make a lot of difference in the conduct of apparently sedate individuals. One of them crashed a bottle of soda water against a wall where it splashed in a gush of foam and called the waiter a pig and promised that the next bottle would land on his head if it arrived as warm as the first.

Pepe Romano and Maria Camargo did a mambo that had the guests clapping wildly, their performance even inflaming the minds of two dashing pilots who jumped up on their table and swigged big draughts from their bottles. Their conduct was a signal. Soon couples were dancing on the table tops and the deer horn chandeliers began to sway slightly.

Romano swayed in his chair. Then he got up. He was well oiled, but after all, it was his birthday. Maria was close to the same condition. Her hair was disheveled and she had lost one of her earrings. Pepe staggered to a table on which rested a large birthday cake, an enormous white frosted one, on which was lettered, To PEPE ON HIS BIRTHDAY. One long candle stuck out of the center. "Friends," Romano grinned, "today I am exactly one year old!"

The crowd cheered loudly and a couple of tables crashed to the floor taking their occupants with them after they had been entangled in a welter of chairs, drinks and tablecloths. Romano wavered in front of one table and was almost beaten to the floor by a barrage of enthusiastic back slapping from the men and moist kisses from the women. Pepe managed to slash the cake into enough fragments to pass around, and it was quite a sight to see chunks of the rich confection being crammed into the mouths of persons who ordinarily would not look at the stuff. I'll bet there were a lot of sick people later.

"Well," said Elena, "how do you like our parties, the wilder kind."

"Good," I said. "We have some like these at home. Only most of them are at night and end up in fights. At least, there hasn't been any here."

"It must be the special list Maria Camargo made up," she said. "The rough characters have been left out."

Patty Parsons threw up her hands and shrugged her shoulders. The Armenian was snoring between two chairs and I saw her looking around. That was Patty all over. If one escort became unsuitable, she'd cast her eyes around for a substitute. The orchestra had already left and the only tables still occupied were by those unable to get to their feet. Ronnie Harper and his blonde gal lay side by side on a long table like a couple of post mortem jobs. The Armenian had sagged to the floor, and Patty Parsons had vanished. Pepe Romano and Maria Camargo had slipped away someplace.

Hetty Telger and her husband were ready to leave. We joined them. "Let's go over to the Hotel Metro for some supper."

It was a good idea. I was hungry. When the stimulation of alcohol wears off you can eat like a horse. We got to the footbridge that led to the parking lot. Not all the drunks were left inside. There were wild yells followed by heavy splashes as unsteady guests tumbled into the lake.

"Step on the gas," said Hetty. "I can smell that food."

Leon was waiting for me downstairs after I'd taken Elena home late in the afternoon. He had a package under his arm. I didn't have to ask him what it contained. I could smell the satisfying aroma of freshly roasted coffee.

We went upstairs and I put a pot on the tiny stove in the small kitchen that also had a diminutive refrigerator.

Leon rubbed his eyes. "I sure could use a few cups of that coffee when it is ready. I had a long day at Headquarters and got orders to pick up Lisa Morel and Max Martellini tomorrow morning for questioning. The boss wants to see them. If they are hiding anything, he will get it out of them. Moran is an old hand at asking questions. Nobody fools him."

Leon yawned as I handed him a cup of coffee. "You know, I think that I'll take a nap. After a second cup. I don't have to go back to Headquarters today and I want to be in good shape tomorrow. But I don't want to sleep until tonight. Wake me up about seven, we'll have something to eat and then go to the wrestling matches." He held up his hands before I could say anything. "Oh, I know they're not on the level but I find them very entertaining."

I didn't want to disturb Leon. He didn't even have a second cup. He had put down a half-filled cup, his first one, and was already snoring on the sofa. So I went out and headed for one of the coffee shops near Plaza San Martin. One cup wasn't enough for me. There was a tap on my arm. It was Elena Remasso. "Did I startle you?" she asked.

"No."

"Didn't you see me? I've been walking across the street for some time."

"No," I said. "When I'm on my way for a cup of coffee, I don't see anybody. I'm a man with a single purpose and completely oblivious of anything around me."

"Even the women?" she laughed. "Do you mind if I join you? I would love a cup of coffee."

Elena Remasso sipped her coffee while I put away a crunchy roll and a slice of Edam cheese. I discovered I was a little hungry. She gazed at me over her cup. "Do you know there is one person in Lima who will be terribly sorry to see you leave here?"

"Who?"

"Me," she said and she looked as if she meant it.

"That's the way it is," I said. "I'm only on a vacation and have to return some time. But I like it here. I've met a lot of nice people."

Elena put her cards right on the table face up. "Have you ever thought of getting married?"

"A number of times. Just didn't meet the right party." I put down my cup. "I thought I met the right one once but it didn't work out."

"Was it a matter of money?" she asked.

"Partly," I said. "What about yourself?"

"These men bore me," she said. "But let us not talk about them. I see enough of them every day." She dismissed that subject quickly. "Do you ever get to Miami Beach?"

"Not unless I get a special assignment. It wouldn't be too hard. California newspapers are always looking for things to write about Florida. We have a sort of a good natured rivalry."

Her eyes brightened. "I go there every year to buy clothes. We could meet there any time you say and be together without all the local gossipers breathing down our necks."

Elena was clever. She had planted the idea and it was up to me to follow-up. I got her a cab at the corner. She had the motel look in her eye, the Miami Beach variety.

I like a good laugh like the next fellow and they tell me a good place for laughs is the open air arena on Avenida Argentina, where they put on night wrestling matches that operate without even the use of scripts. Every bare spot on the adobe walls surrounding whole blocks was plastered with bills and colored posters advertising the 'championship' match between *El Oso* and *El Yanqui*. The Bear was covered with enough hair to upholster the leather chairs in a men's club. The "Yankee" was a blonde Chilean, whose hair was bleached to a straw color by a combination of beach sun and peroxide. All Yankees are supposed to be blonde with blue eyes, so the Chilean was a Yankee by virtue of his hair. It was rather vague as to what 'championship' was at stake although the Bear claimed to be king of most of southern Peru and some of the northern provinces, except Tumbes, over which a wiry Ecuadorian named Pablo Benevente held sway, claiming that the Bear was afraid to meet him. The truth of the matter was that the stakes in that arena were too small to bother with and the climate too hot for sweating behemoths. The Chilean was supposed to be champion in his own country but his status had been challenged by a rival faction which had its own man. He and El Yanqui had met previously with the blonde claiming a foul although the winning fall was awarded to his opponent. Now he was building up his reputation for a re-match.

I got a couple of tickets at a broken-down booth and Leon picked out a wooden bench that was literally sprinkled with splinters.

"Nice spot you selected," I said, knocking out some of the splinters with a rolled-up newspaper.

"Sit on your newspaper, *amigo*," he said. Leon felt of the bench gingerly, spread out his newspaper and sat down.

The Bear came out first, his big chest sprouting hair that hung over a sweat-stained, faded purple robe. He held his arms over his head, walked to all four corners of the ring and then sat down on a stool. El Yanqui followed him into the ring. The Chilean was a good-looking guy. With his tanned face and yellow hair he resembled the fellow they use on those fancy posters to advertise the ski resorts in the Austrian Tyrol. He reached down into a bucket and took a swig of cold wine, rolled it around his lips, and then swallowed it. The Bear in the opposite corner licked his lips as if he were tasting the wine and looked appealingly at the Chilean, who, if he were a gentleman, would have passed the bottle across the ring."

The first fall was a quick one. Apparently, the Bear was chagrined by not being offered a sip of wine and roared across the ring. Before the Chilean could get set, he was thrown heavily to the mat and pinned flat on his back. The crowd booed, stamped their feet and began to throw papers and debris into the ring. The gladiators went back to their corners and a man climbed into the ring.

"Please, gentlemen," he requested. "I ask you not to throw anything in the ring. You may hurt the wrestlers. They cannot function properly if you hurl missiles at them." He turned a sorrowful face at the spectators and crawled through the ropes.

The Chilean had another sip of wine and came back with fury in his eyes.

He tore out a handfull of the Bear's chest hair and stamped on it, then tripped him and got a scissors grip across his body. The Bear got out of that one and the Chilean tried a spread-eagle, the Bear groaning and beating his huge fists on the canvas. This went on for about ten minutes with the tide swaying in favor of the Chilean for a while and then back to thè Bear. At the half-hour mark, the Chilean got the Bear in a flying mare and flipped him down like a bag of cement. The air seemed to go out of his hairy opponent and the Chilean landed right on his heaving stomach. The falls stood at one all.

The time limit for the third fall was an agreed upon eleven o'clock deadline and at that time the boys were still snorting and groaning. The bout was called a draw and a re-match for the following was announced.

We extricated ourselves from the splinters and newspapers and headed for the dusty alley that led to the street. Leon kept scratching at his back. "Something is itching the hell out of me *amigo*," he said. "This place must be loaded with fleas."

I looked at his jacket. Something black was sticking out of it like a small knob. It was a knife handle.

"My God!" I yelled. "You've been stabbed!"

A small knife, with a black rubber handle, stuck from under his left shoulder, looking like a black bug against his coat. Leon unbuttoned his shirt. The thin blade of the knife was inserted under the skin like a letter opener under the flap of an envelope. It was more like an icepick than a knife and Leon came close to having his heart skewered on the thing which was apparently a devilishly home-made weapon. But what was just as unusual was the absence of bleeding from the wound. The blood had collected under the skin and the wound had started to purple.

"One of the neatest incisions I have ever seen," said Leon lifting up his arm. "A few inches higher and I would have been finished, right through the heart."

We drove to Headquarters. Dr. Lopez wasn't around but his assistant did a good job. He put a pad on the incision after cleaning it up and told Leon to come back the next day for a fresh dressing. We went across the street to the Cafe Espana and had a quick brandy.

On our way out of the cafe, Leon noticed that there was a light burning in Director-General Moran's office. "There must be something up," he said. "Moran rarely works as late as midnight."

Inspector-General Moran was at his desk. An ashtray filled with ground out cigarette butts was in front of him. The room was blue with smoke. Moran put the phone back on its base. "Ah! Leon," he said, "you must be psychic. I wanted you and here you are. I have been calling your home, several bars and a number of theaters without any success and here you step right into my office. How did you know I was here?"

"The light in the window," said Leon. "I dropped in on Dr. Lopez to get patched up. Somebody stabbed me at the wrestling matches tonight."

"You shouldn't go to such places if they are so dangerous," smiled Moran. "Was it bad?"

"Just lost a little skin," said Leon, "and practically no blood at all."

"I'm glad to hear that," said Moran. "Now to the business we have. I had Max Martellini and Lisa Morel picked up tonight."

Leon looked surprised. Moran put up his hand. "I know you were detailed to get them tomorrow but at the last moment I decided that tonight would be better. Night is the best time to pick up suspects. They are usually tired and less apt to lie. They are also thrown off guard and do not have the time to conceal anything, if they have something around they wish to hide. Now I plan to hold both of them here as long as I can on suspicion of smuggling gold out of the country, which, of course, they will both deny. But this will give me the time I need before their lawyers come knocking at my door. Both of them probably know more about the Barkovit murder than they pretend to know. Barkovit is the key. When we find out who killed him, we will have the murderer of the rest as well. Did you know that the late Mr. Barkovit was Lisa Morel's brother-in-law?"

"Yes," Leon said.

Moran lit another cigarette. "Actually both of them have been smugglers. They worked together getting emeralds out of Brazil about fifteen years ago. By morning they should be able to talk. They won't get anything to eat until they have answered a few questions. By the way, do you think that Martellini may have stabbed you?"

"No," said Leon shaking his head. "He doesn't have the guts. And I don't think that Lisa Morel hired anybody to do the job, either. She knows she's *persona non grata* with us."

Moran tapped his cigarette on the edge of the ashtray. "Well, gentlemen, I am going home. There are extra straw mattresses here but I have a very comfortable bed at my house."

CHAPTER EIGHT

AN AUTO HORN honked outside my window. I looked out. There was a black Lincoln Continental at the curb. Hetty Telger looked up and waved her arms. "Come down," she said. It was one of those cloudy, gloomy mornings, the kind of day you'd like to stay in your own apartment and talk about old silver, ceramics and antique firearms with a girl who had a receptive disposition.

Hetty's husband was at the wheel. Hetty introduced me to her friend in the back seat, a Canadian woman named Rowena Chalmers, an artist who was illustrating and writing a book on ancient textiles. Rowena carried a sketchbook and a couple of pencils fastened with an elastic band.

"We're on our way to the Archaeological Museum," said Hetty. "You can take us around. I know you'll be interested in a lot of things there." Show them around? Hetty must have been there dozens of times. I hadn't been there once. Her husband smiled. I could see him on his way to the Club Excelsior for a dice shaking session with his friends after dropping us off at the museum.

The National Museum of Archaeology and Anthoropology stood in an old section of the city known as *Magdalena Vieja* and was built by the Peruvian Government to house a great collection of pre-Inca and Inca ceramics, textiles and stone carvings. It was close to the old church of *Magdalena Vieja* in the Plaza Bolivar, one of the most perfect of the Colonial churches, both buildings being close to small houses of another century that gave the section a charm of antiquity. The front of the museum looked like the entrance to an Inca temple with its carefully fitted stonework and carved archway of mythical beasts. There was a visitor's book inside the entrance with names of persons from all over the world.

The center was an open patio paved with red tiles on which rested grotesque carved figures, monoliths and strange appearing slabs. On the four corners were arranged glass cases containing ceramics excavated from the graveyards that dot the Peruvian coast, Chimu from the ancient fortress city of Chan-Chan near the present city of Trujillo in northern Peru, and distinguished by their gray-black color, red figures and jars from Chancay and Paracas and others from civilizations that existed long before the sway of the Imperial Empire of the Incas.

Professor Reimer was scrutinizing the contents of a corner case. Hetty Telger knew him. There were few persons of any prominence in Lima that she did not know. The Professor tipped his black fedora to the ladies.

The Professor pointed out a jar in the form of a man's head. "This is something unusual. If you come closer you will see what I mean." We moved closer.

"Examine that face," said Professor Reimer. "Note the eyes, cheekbones and the shape of the skull. Definitely Caucasian. Not a trace of the Indian in that face. That one came from Chancay and it completely refutes the theory that the Indians here were of a Mongoloid strain. I wouldn't be at all surprised if the person depicted there was a member of a dead race, long extinct before the Incas appeared on the scene. It is a subject worthy of further investigation and one with tremendous possibilities."

Professor Reimer suddenly pulled a big gold watch from his pocket. "I have almost forgotten," he said. "I have an appointment with the curator here to unlock one of those large cases in the back section of the museum. There are some items there I would like to see in more detail. I am doing a special paper for the University and it must be ready by next Saturday." He tipped his black fedora and walked to the back of the museum.

Rowena Chalmers had brought along a small box camera with which she photographed several of the mummies found in the desert cemeteries clothed in fabrics covered with designs that still looked bright and fresh. The dyes were of vegetable origin and some of the colors have not been duplicated since even with the available knowledge of modern day chemistry. She was also rapidly filling her sketchbook with drawings of the fragments of cloth that lay in cases, carefully indicating the colors. Her work was now completed in the textile section and she told Hetty she would like to see some of the other items, like the statues and slabs in the open patio. Hetty insisted that we take photos of ourselves. "Let's take some shots of that big idol in the patio," she said. "We'll stand in front of it and you can tell your friends that you dug it up. Who is going to dispute it with you?"

It was like posing in front of a big fish that somebody else caught, but anything to please Hetty. The stone idol, probably dragged from its resting place by Pizarro's conquistadores, was in a state of disrepair but reconstruction was almost completed. Cracks that ran halfway down the body had been cleverly filled with cement of the same shade of color as the stone. The fifteen foot idol weighed over ten tons and was propped up in back by two heavy logs to hold the sections securely together until the cement set.

Hetty pulled me in front of the statue and twined her arm around mine. "Now," she said, "isn't this nice? Of course, don't tell your friends that you dug me up at the same time." Hetty patted her hair and smiled. I smiled, too, but it was a short one. There was an ominous crack. "Look out!" Hetty shrieked and pulled me forward away from the toppling monster which crashed with a roar and a rain of fragments that splattered against the glass covered cases like buckshot. Hetty landed right in my lap and she must have loved every moment of it.

Hetty squeezed my hand. "I'm thankful you were with me," I said. "In another split second I would have been flatter than one of those pounded steaks they serve at the Lido."

We looked at Rowena Chalmers. The lady was chalky white and frozen in the same spot from which she started to focus the camera. She was so rigid with fright that she could have been carried into the next room, dressed in one of the costumes shed by the mummies, and gotten by as a genuine model of a 3,000 year old spring outfit—preMolyneaux, Dior and Dache.

The crash also brought a number of the museum employees and a few tourists to the scene as well as the curator, Emilio Contreras, who rushed out of his office to find out what the hell was going on in an otherwise tranquil atmosphere where you could hear a pin drop.

Contreras surveyed the ruin and threw his hands over his face." *Por Dios!*" he yelled. "What has happened?" Then he saw me standing on the edge of the debris looking cool and unshaken and I could visualize what was churning around in his mind. These foreigners, they are so clumsy, and this one, this indifferent one, he must have pushed over the idol to see what was underneath. He glared at me and I expected him to rush back to his office and make out a bill for a couple of million dollars.

"Senor!" he stormed. "What have you done here? This idol, it is irreplaceable, the only one in the world. What will happen now? I am ruined!" He clapped his hands over his head and began to pull at his sparse hair. "I must have your name, Senor."

Contreras calmed down a bit. "Oh, Senora Telger. This man. He has ruined this magnificent idol."

"My friend has been with me all the time since we came here," said Hetty. "How could he possibly push over this heavy thing? The sign said it weighed more than ten tons. Do you think he tried to kill himself and me at the same time? Take a good look at the back of what is left of that stone idol."

The heavy logs that formerly supported the idol lay in the pile of splintered stone. Each had a length of rope tied around an end.

It was a very simple but effective arrangement. While we stood in front of the idol, it seemed, somebody had yanked on the ropes.

Contreras was aghast. "Did somebody try to murder you?"

"Not Senora Telger," I said. "Me."

"Why should they?" asked Contreras.

"That's a long story and I don't have the time to tell it in detail," I said.

We headed for the street and some fresh air, air without the added ingredient of stone dust. We walked about the narrow streets with little conversation. The sight of a black Lincoln Continental was a welcome one.

"You know, Hetty," I said on the way back to the center of Lima, "your house is the safest place in town. What could possibly happen there?"

"That depends on what you are doing," she said.

"Amigo, I have some news for you," said Leon, making a late morning visit.

"What happened to you?" I asked. "Did you win the Lima-Callao lottery? I have news for you, too. Hetty Telger and myself almost got flattened by a ten ton idol at the Archaelogical Museum about a half hour ago."

"Eh!" said Leon. "I'll listen to that later." He slapped me on the back. "A night on those straw mattresses at the jail apparently changed the minds of Lisa Morel and Max Martellini. Max didn't have much to say that amounted to anything we already didn't know. But Lisa surprised even Moran. She started to talk. She said that her luck had been so bad it couldn't get any worse by telling Moran what he wanted.

"Lisa's place, as you know, has been closed now for over six months and the bills were piling up. Remember when you saw her place? I don't know how much you looked around but I examined that downstairs room minutely. There wasn't a single antique piece in the room. Everything was modern. That's what put me on her trace when I saw her visiting Martellini's shop. She wasn't buying on those trips. She was after something else."

"What was that?"

"I'll come to that," said Leon. He snapped a cigarette into his mouth and scratched a match. "Moran politely asked Lisa what she was doing in Martellini's office. Moran can be very polite when he wants to and besides he had just had coffee served. After a hot cup, Lisa admitted that she hadn't seen Max for over a year before the first visit to the shop. All she wanted, she said, was the two thousand dollars she had loaned Max to keep his business from going on the rocks. His business was bad, she said, because after you sell Peru's fifty wealthy families, who else is there to sell to? Max carries expensive items and there is a lot of truth in that statement.

"Max didn't have the money he owed her, she said, but he had a brilliant idea. Why not blackmail somebody? Say, for about ten thousand dollars and split fifty-fifty. Lisa would not only get her money back but with a profit of three thousand dollars more on the deal. Of course, neither of them could approach the intended victim and make the demands. But Lisa had just the man for the job. Her brother-in-law Josef Barkovit. Josef had been in so many slimy businesses with Lisa before that he agreed to do the job."

"How much was he getting paid for it?"

"Five hundred dollars," said Leon.

"Lisa certainly was generous," I said.

"She really is generous," said Leon. "To herself."

"Who was the victim for the shake-down? Some rich guy who talked a little too much during one of Lisa's parties?"

"We don't know that yet," said Leon, "but by the time that Moran gets through with her he will know how many cavities she has in her teeth."

The phone rang. "You can take me to lunch, now I've calmed down," said Hetty Telger. "Wasn't it thoughtful of me to call you?"

"Very," I said. "I'll take you along if you promise not to order anything more expensive than the five sole special at the Cafe Algeria."

"You just be careful what you say," she laughed. "I might ask for a package of cigarettes and run the bill up to ten soles."

"I'm not trying to be economical," I said. "Just thinking about your figure. As a matter of fact, I think about it all the time."

"Go on!" she said. "With a line like that to listen to I won't eat a thing. Perhaps just a cup of coffee."

I hung up the phone. "See you later," I said to Leon. "Have to go out."

"Hetty Telger?" he asked.

"Right."

"What does she see in you anyway?"

"She likes big green eyes," I said.

The Cafe Algeria didn't even have an oasis. It was located on a side street off Carabaya to keep a good distance away from cafes with names originating in the countries on the sandy shores of North Africa like El Libya, El Tunisia and the Morocco. The Cafe Algeria didn't even serve skewered lamb broiled over charcoal like some of the other restaurants. It was different. It served ham and eggs and bacon and eggs, one of the few places in the city that specialized in these dishes, and coffee, American style. The nearest thing to the desert was not the name of the place but the appearance of the proprietor who had a dark complexion and a long mustache. He looked like an Arab but he was a Czech named Franz.

Hetty had already selected a table near the entrance facing the street. It was one of those places without a front door. You stepped inside and got your own location.

"This is a good spot," I said. "It has a perfect view of the street and I can see all the women walking by."

"I'm glad you're satisfied with the location," she said. "But it is a little away from the entrance. If you said something they wouldn't hear you anyway."

"You mean if I tossed a few remarks in their direction?"

Hetty looked surprised. "Don't tell me that you're doing that now?"

"Got a few pointers in front of the Aero Club. It was a very enjoyable experience."

"Don't try that technique when you go home to the States," she said. "The girls might not understand."

Hetty didn't eat very much. She nibbled at her sandwich and dawdled over her coffee. Other things seemed to occupy her mind. She pushed away the dishes in front of her and reached for a cigarette.

"When are you returning home?" she asked. "Have you had your fill of this place yet?"

"In a month, maybe," I said. "Can't say that I've been bored. I haven't even had time to think. People have been really wonderful."

"I wish I could say that," she said. "I'd like to leave myself. I've been here for years and I hate the place." She looked up sorrowfully. "One can't have everything."

"You could take a trip out of the country once in a while," I suggested. "It might give you a new outlook on things."

"That's just the trouble," she said. "After being in other places and comparing things and then coming back with a new outlook, I'd be worse off than I am now."

Hetty reached into her purse and took out a mirror and fiddled with her hair. There was something else that came out of her bag with the mirror. It was a key. She slid it towards me under her napkin. "Try it out tonight at seven. But be sure to be on time." She gave me an address of an apartment building in Chorrillos.

I got a cab from Plaza San Martin and at five to seven stopped near the Chorrillos Theater, a square white building with the name sprawled across the entire front in black script. The apartment building was only two blocks away and I walked down the narrow street paved with cobblestones and lined on both sides with white oaks.

The apartment was on the second floor. I grated the key in the lock and pushed open the door. The one large room was practically bare of furniture. A lone watercolor hung on a long expanse of wall, there was one chair and a small table, and the main item, the bed. The bed looked comfortable and Hetty was sitting on the edge with her shoes on the floor and her gray, tailored suit half off her back. There was a bottle of brandy and a glass on the small table. Hetty had started off the evening in good form.

I sat down on the bed and she twined her arms around my neck and pulled me back on the pillow. Her face lay against mine and seemed to burn right through me. She kissed me so hard that she bit my lip and the salty taste of blood welled into my mouth. Her breathing came in short, irregular bursts and she melted into my embrace and I seemed to be floating into space.

Afterward I reached over the edge of the bed to the floor where my jacket and shoes and other assorted items of clothing were strewn and got a cigarette. I lit it and Hetty took a long draw exhaling the smoke in a satisfied sigh. She handed it back to me.

"Take me with you when you go back," she pleaded. "Please take me!"

"That's impossible, you know that. Be reasonable."

"I am being reasonable," she insisted. "I just can't stand this place any longer and I want to get away as quickly as possible."

"You just can't pick yourself up and leave here like this."

"Yes, I can," she said. "I want to go with you. I have enough money to pay for my own plane ticket and plenty left over after that. Please?"

"I can't."

"You must!" She punched hard with clenched fists against my chest. Her small hands opened and long nails tore at my neck.

"Take me!"

It was useless to stay any longer. Hetty was sobbing hysterically. "You beasts!" she screamed. "All of you, beasts, beasts, beasts!"

The key was still in the lock where I had left it. I could hear Hetty on the other side of the door. The sound was not a pleasant one to listen to.

There was a car at the curb and a familiar figure was getting out. It was the doctor with the Cesar Romero look and the even, white wolf teeth. He had a long chain in his hand and was twirling a key at the end of it. The flashing arc stopped and I got a look at the key. It was a brother of the one in the lock of the apartment door upstairs. He saw me and came closer. "Hola," he said and patted me on the back, sneaking a look at the window of the apartment at the same time. The window was dark. The doctor threw back his head and laughed loudly, his white teeth gleaming in the light of the street lamp. I managed a half-hearted smile. It could have been a funny situation, funny, but not laughable.

The doctor slapped me on the back again. "*Es la vida!*" he said. He looked up at the window. It was still dark. He threw up his hands in resignation, got into the car, and pulled away from the curb. I looked up at the building. Nothing seemed to stir anyplace. In a few minutes the upper floors were shrouded in mist. I walked back to the Chorillos Theater and got a cab and told the driver to take me to Plaza San Martin.

I got out at the Plaza and went into a coffee shop for something hot. It was getting clammy outside. Elena Remasso was sitting at a table with a dark girl with long hair.

"Hello!" she said. "Roberto, my friend Elvira Castillo." The girl nodded her head and smiled. Elena Remasso and Elvira Castillo got up.

"Going?" I asked.

"Yes," said Elena. "I wish I could have some coffee with you but we have to leave. My car is being repaired and the last bus leaves here in a few moments."

I walked them to the Miradores bus stop. The bus was just pulling around the corner.

"Did you go to the *cine,* tonight?" she asked.

"Yes," I lied.

"How was the performance?"

"Wonderful," I said. I didn't lie this time.

"By the way," she said, "I will get in touch with you tomorrow. The *Carnavales* will be starting and there will be a lot of good parties around."

"Thanks," I said. The bus drew away and I made a second try for that cup of coffee.

CHAPTER NINE

I N ONE DAY the *Carnavales* had taken over Lima. It was the spot on the calendar when the city was governed by the spirit of revelry and bufoonry and a time when you could tell the cop on the corner to go to hell and he would take it in a good-natured manner. Most of the stores were already closed and wise shoppers had previously purchased a good supply of bread as even the bakers had deserted the ovens and kept them on low heat only to bake some of the special pastries for the occasion.

If you had no place to go, it was a good idea to hole up in your own apartment with a pleasant companion, a good stock of brandy and enough food to last for the period of the holiday. It was somewhat hazardous to walk the streets. You could be assailed from both the pavements and the buildings. Giggling girls wearing black masks hurled bags of flour or water and sometimes bags containing something else out of windows. If you got too close to the buildings, you were also a prime subject for the pickpockets who lurked in the doorways. Feigning drunkenness, they would lurch out, grab you by the lapels of your jacket and wish you a happy holiday while picking your pocket clean.

The middle of the street was just as bad. Although there wasn't much traffic, there was no scarcity of drunken drivers who regarded pedestrians as open season prey. And groups of revelers roamed the streets carrying atomizers loaded with cheap perfume which they sprayed on everybody they met. That wasn't too bad. All that could happen was that you smelled like the stuff that sells for about a dollar a quart, and your clothes would take several cleanings to get rid of the aroma. But other, more sadistic individuals carried syringes filled with ether to squirt in the eyes of their victims. To counter the ether spray, a number of persons wore hoods and plastic shields over their faces. It was certainly a hell of a lot better to stay in your own apartment with a girl whom you made promise not to dab perfume in back of your ears or hit you with a bag of water.

A cousin of Elena's was having a big party in a place over in Miraflores so we went over, arriving at the house at eight o'clock with a lot of activity already in progress. There was a garden in back of the house with dangling lanterns festooned with streamers of colored crepe paper stretched across criss-crossed ropes over plenty of tables. The bar in the corner was well stocked with a good assortment to make anybody forget where he was after a while. Elena's cousin didn't have any vineyards, cotton or sugar plantations, but her family did have a couple of copper mines tucked away in the pantry.

Pepe Romano was mixing drinks at the bar. "Hola, pal," he said. "They don't need a bartender with me around. I can mix any drink in the book." Nobody tried to test Pepe's knowledge of mixing drinks. Most of the stuff poured was either scotch or brandy. He handed me a scotch and soda. I almost gagged. It must have been a triple scotch.

"What are you trying to do, get me drunk?" I asked. "Remember, I just got here."

"Sure, why not," said Romano. "It is only eight-thirty now. By midnight this place should be jumping. Have you any objections?"

The place was jumping a long time before midnight. Romano had long been replaced by several amateur bartenders and was nowhere in sight. The air was filled with streamers of crepe paper and billowing clouds of confetti. The Armenian was snoring on a sofa with a paper hat covering his face. A wag had placed a bouquet of flowers on his chest. I didn't see Patty Parsons around but I had an idea that she was someplace with one of the airline pilots. She must have disowned the Armenian.

After a while, most of the couples in the place had filtered into other parts of the house and the garden and there were only a few dancers remaining in the big living room. Elena's cousin was dancing with Hernando Davila, the announcer at Radio Luna. She looked a little like Elena but didn't have her figure or her personality. Her mother was sitting at the end of the room keeping a watchful eye on her little Luisa and waiting to close up the place for the evening. The old lady was still as fresh as a daisy. Of course, she didn't drink anything, but with a natural vitality like that, I was sure she would live to be a hundred.

The coffee shops in Miraflores were closed so we drove to Plaza San Martin. Elena had her little Austin-Healey this time. She parked the shiny, red sportster in front of the Hotel Europa and we headed for one of those cafes on Jiron Union, a place run by an Italian chain of coffee outfits that specialized in brewing the drink in the espresso style.

Jiron Union, Lima's main street, starts near the Plaza San Martin and ends at the Cathedral and the fountain surrounded by griffons and dragon-faced beasts at the Plaza de Armes, an archway of jutting balconies and signs, an overhead collection of chaos, accentuates the narrowness of the streets. The section was neon happy and night brought out every color of the spectrum. Under the tangle of signs are shops specializing in Peruvian silver, rugs, and the softest, most sensuous feeling bed coverings made from the fleece of the vicuna. A celestial spread of this kind usually evokes paeans of praise from women and smart travelers usually grab up the best ones for their wives and best girls. However, those made from the finer-matched skins are scarce as the government limits the hunting of the fleet animal to keep it from becoming extinct. Nearby shops displayed hand-tooled, leather-covered chairs, tables and stools, dotted with bronze fasteners and covered with designs in the motif of the vanished

Viceregal period. Drug stores are located every few steps, well stocked with the latest in antibiotics, headache remedies, reducing aids and preparations designed to combat all the ailments to which man is heir.

There was a bronze map of the world on the wall of the Cafe Florencia that showed the location of similar shops in the chain in different countries. The headquarters of the organization was located in Milan and was indicated by a large star. A waiter brought in a tray of freshly ground coffee and handed it to a man in back of the large, shining espresso making machines, that looked like a boiler. The delicious odor filled the place with a satisfying wave of goodness that must have tickled the noses of every person in the place. The coffee was dark, almost black, a deep roast, even darker than the French roast, and made by the Italian method for use in the brewing machine that makes the coffee by drawing live steam through the coal-black roasted grains, one cup at a time.

Elena had a *cappuccino,* which was an addition of hot milk, cinnamon and whipped cream to the espresso, a typical ladies' drink. I sipped my drink but only got halfway through the cup. There was a roar outside that seemed to grow in intensity like a gathering thunder storm that had rolled in from a distant point. I had visions of an impending earthquake. I threw some money on the counter, grabbed Elena by the arm, and we ran to the doorway. A couple of waiters followed us. To the devil with the customers!

There was a milling crowd in front of the corner of Union and Yupanqui, a mob that began to swell with the *Carnivales* revelers that streamed in from the direction of Plaza San Martin where most of the large hotels were situated. The reason soon became apparent. A full-scale stake-out was in session, conducted in the best fashion of the vice squad of the Los Angeles Police, and all the streets close by were sealed off tighter than the lid on a jar of Grandma's strawberry jam. Brand new black Ford sedans were bristling with members of the *Guardia Civil* carrying shiny 9mm machine pistols and soldiers with Mauser rifles. A captain of police stood in a doorway brandishing a pearl-handled .38 Smith & Wesson and politely motioned pedestrians to turn around and go back just where they had come from. Number 765, where the captain stood was crawling with police who filled the long, dank corridor. Across the street in a building covered with big yellow scales of peeling paint, more policemen hung out of the windows waiting for something to happen.

We saw Leon on the edge of the thinning crowd that was being dispersed by the police. He had his left arm in a sling. His face was pale.

"What happened to you?" I asked. "Get hit by a cab?"

"It's Pepe Romano!" yelled Leon grabbing me with his good arm. "He's somewhere in this building. They're searching the place from top to bottom."

"Romano? Has he gone loco?"

"Maybe he has," said Leon. "Moran called me about an hour ago. Lisa Morel and Max Martellini cracked wide open. They spilled everything. Max had told Lisa about the drug traffic he was carrying on with Pepe Romano. Professor Reimer was their source of supply. Lisa was overcome with greed and they decided to put the screws on Pepe Romano and use Barkovit for the hatchet man. Both she and Max swear that neither of them had anything to do with Barkovit's murder. They think Romano did the job. They may be right. Moran told me to pick up . Romano at his house for questioning, so I went there but there was nobody at home."

"But we saw Romano tonight," I said. "He was at a party with us at Miraflores."

"That must have been several hours ago," said Leon.

I agreed with him. "As a matter of fact, I don't remember seeing him around after ten o'clock."

"I took a chance and went to his office. There was nobody in there, either, so I went over to the warehouse which is in back of the building. I almost fell over Romano and he dropped a package he was carrying, pulled out a gun and shot me in the shoulder. Luckily it was only a flesh wound. The package Romano dropped is now over at the police laboratory. They think it holds about fifty-thousand dollars worth of cocaine. We lost track of Romano for about two hours until he was seen entering this building. Romano will have a hard time getting away. Everybody knows him and will easily recognize him."

"Have the police covered the back entrances?"

"There are none as far as we can make out. But this area is a maze of tunnels. These old time architects may have had escape routes in mind when they put up these buildings. Those were violent times. This is a former residence and it has more doorways, halls and passageways than you can imagine. And besides, Romano knows every alley and hole in this town. He was born here."

The building was combed from damp cellar to the dusty roof covered with droppings from the black turkey buzzards, who represent the unofficial sanitation department of Lima. Romano had flown the coop, broken through the thin plaster that covered an old doorway and came up safe and sound in the kitchen of the Napoli Restaurant, nodding in recognition to the head waiter on the way out to the street.

But the closeness of the buildings, practically piled on top of each other, provided a trap as effective as the stake-out of the police. Despite the abundance of rabbit warrens there was little place to hide without being seen by somebody in the heavily populated section of the teeming city.

Romano was slowly edging his way to the rim of the city in an effort to get to the suburbs, where there was plenty of space and a place to stay until he could sneak south and get into either Bolivia or Chile. After these places, there were other countries if it became too hot for him, especially Buenos Aires, where he could lose himself in Argentina's biggest city. And Pepe would have made it, too, if fate had not intervened. He was seen emerging from the ancient vaults that once lay under the monastery of the Church of the Encarnacion, over which towers a modern office building. Few persons knew of the existence of the vaults found only on yellowed plans of the city, but Romano did, entering them at the Plaza San Martin through a ventilator and walking through the other end, part of which was used as a truck maintenance section by a firm importing mining machinery.

We saw Guillermo Perez of the police pistol team running to the end of Plaza San Martin. We could see nothing as Perez fired at a moving shadow that appeared from behind a column in front of a coffee shop, wavered and then became part of the darkness. Perez was one of the best shots in the country and he didn't miss.

It was cool and the blood that oozed into the gutter soon congealed into a rusty red rope. A woman who pushed her way through the crowd to get a better look screamed when a leg jerked convulsively and an arm quivered. But Pepe wasn't trying to get up. He couldn't anyway. He was as dead as a corvina that had been caught the day before.

Romano was loaded into the old meat wagon that always had the same destination, the morgue. Leon shook his head and reached for a cigarette. He was fumbling around with his one good arm and I handed him one of mine and snapped a match in front of it. "Too bad," Leon said taking a long drag and blowing two jets of smoke through his nostrils, "Romano was really a nice fellow. You got to know him fairly well, didn't you?"

I shrugged.

"It is amazing how many cocaine addicts there are in Lima," said Leon. "Many of them come from the best families, were well-educated in places like Paris, London and the States, and it is hard to figure them out. Perhaps their addiction is the product of boredom, although it is hard to visualize how people with money can become bored. I know I could find plenty to do if I had a sufficient supply of cash." He threw down his cigarette and ground it under his heel. "But what is just as unusual is that most of the addicts are known. Due to their high social positions and money they are never bothered, even though it is due to them that the traffic flourishes. After all, there must be customers for the stuff. For example, I could name you several like Francisco Gonzales, who owns one of the largest publishing companies here and keeps a young painter in a suite of rooms at the Hotel Europa."

"How did Romano fit into this puzzle?" I asked. "I know that Martellini's shop was used as a salesroom for the stuff brought there by Professor Reimer. I still don't see where he came in."

"Romano was in desperate circumstances financially," said Leon. "That picture he made flopped right in the cutting room. Of course, Maria Camargo knew nothing about that. Pepe kept it quiet. In addition, by living over his head, he had squandered all the money she had put into future productions, and Pepe owed plenty. Movie equipment is expensive. Had she learned what had happened, she would have saved us the trouble of shooting him.

"Anyway, one morning Romano saw Francisco Gonzalez, whom he knew used to take a sniff or two with his morning coffee, come out of Martellini's shop. This was not unusual although Gonzales is not regarded as a lover of art objects. But when these visits were repeated week after week, Romano put two and two together. He was next door to Martellini, you know, so one day he saw Max and put his cards right on the table and told Max he wanted to get into the deal he was certain existed. There was no use trying to bluff. Martellini decided that Pepe was a safe risk and wouldn't give the deal away to the police. There was nothing else he could do. After all, what was one more partner. Professor Reimer grumbled when he heard about the new partner but he got used to the idea. Pepe was a pleasant fellow and what better place to keep the stuff than in the old warehouse in back of Romano's place that was never used.

"Coca is a native of Peru," said Leon, "and cocaine is made from the nice shiny green leaves that grow on the slopes of the Andes. If you saw growing coca plants, you'd think they were tea bushes. The Indians who work in the mines at high altitudes chew coca and you can almost always find their cheeks bulging with a wad of the stuff. It makes them insensible to cold and hunger but it also causes deterioration of the liver in time so don't try to take up the habit.

"Professor Reimer was surrounded by archaeological treasures worth a small fortune but he had a mania for possessing things that he would not sell and the state of his income was rapidly becoming serious, so he looked for another source of income. He stocked a supply of crude cocaine which was partially rectified by Zoltan Nebroslava, a Yugoslav chemist who grew the stuff on his farm near Pisac. Carlos Lento, on his excursions to the mountains, would pick up a load and bring it to Reimer, an amateur chemist, who put the finishing touches on the drug in his laboratory. You should have seen his set-up. It is almost as good as the one we have in the police laboratory at Headquarters."

"What about Barkovit? You haven't forgotten all about him in the excitement about Romano, have you?"

"Romano killed Barkovit," said Leon, "and started a string of similar disposals. We know that Barkovit tried to blackmail Romano, probably threatening to tell the police if he didn't come across. Of course, he wasn't going to tell the police anything. The drug traffic was too good and besides exposure would also reveal the others in the business. Apparently, Romano agreed to meet Barkovit on the docks at Callao where it was quiet at the time and then strangled him between the piles of crates. They must have talked a long time. The murder scene was loaded with cigarette butts. Barkovit's. His finger prints were on all of them. Romano, in case you don't know it, was a former 'futbol' player in addition to having a talent for playing the piano. He had the strongest pair of hands I have ever seen.

"Number two for Romano was Graciela Salinas. I don't think that Pepe intended to kill her. She practically asked for it. Graciela found out about Romano's business sideline just a few days before Barkovit was disposed of. Barkovit was a tightwad but when he had wornen around he really opened his wallet and was supplying Graciela with the dresses and shoes that you saw in Patty Parson's apartment. Remember, you told me that Barkovit was one of her good customers? Graciela could never dress the way she did on her salary. Of course, she was playing him for a sucker.

"Barkovit never drank anything stronger than vermouth but one night he went completely off the hook and lapped up a lot of brandy. I got that from one of the boys who hung around El Patio. He was probably anticipating taking Pepe Romano for a real boob. In his drunken mind he thought he was a big man and blurted out what he was going to do with Romano. Graciela just listened with those sharp ears. What she heard was her death warrant. Then she got real greedy. After Barkovit was killed, she decided she had two strikes on Pepe Romano. But she didn't want any money or have him put out of the way. She wanted to marry him. That's what the girls in the beauty salon where she worked told me. They said that Graciela practically swooned when she saw Romano on the street. But he never looked at her. What she didn't know was that Pepe wanted to marry Maria Camargo, who had plenty of money to go along with her figure and looks while Graciela had a nice face and figure but not a sole in the bank. So Pepe broke her pretty neck last week on the bridge when she became too insistent and disposed of her shapely carcass in the river hoping that the rising waters from the mountains would wash her into the Pacific as food for the fish in the Humboldt Current. After all, what was one more murder with Maria Camargo and her money practically in the palm of his hand?"

"Any ideas about what she was doing going through my pockets the night I saw her?" I said. "She wasn't looking for a train schedule."

Leon laughed loudly. "Graciela knew you were a newspaper-man and thought you might have written down what was known about the Barkovit murder. She knew you were with me most of the time and thought you may have come across some valuable information. She was just an inquisitive dame, that's all, and didn't care what she did as long as she accomplished what she was after.

"The murder of Carlos Lento was a mistake, if you want to call it that. It might have been avoided if Romano hadn't been so jumpy. In fact, it was the first indication that he was starting to crack. Business was very good with Lento. He was enjoying himself for the first time in his life and went on a pisco diet. When he ran out of money, he barged into Reimer's house, just at the very moment when the Professor and Romano were counting the week's receipts. Reimer tried to push the money under the table-cloth, but Lento, even in his drunken state, saw the money and demanded a loan. The Professor pushed a fifty sole note towards him but he demanded more and was getting louder all the time. There was a policeman's beat near the house and Romano was getting more exasperated all the time. When Lento lunged for the cash on the table, Romano snatched a cord from a window drape and pulled it around his throat. He only meant to quiet Lento but he didn't know the strength in those big hands of his and probably pulled a little too hard on the cord. It must have been too much pisco and too much rope but the fat man was dead. There was nothing else to do but dispose of the body and it had to be done fast. Looking outside the window to make sure the police-man was not around, they loaded Lento into the Professor's little Renault and later dumped him in fogbound Miraflores, where he lived, to make it appear that he was probably the victim of one of his drinking companions. Professor Reimer gave every detail of what happened in that room. For the first time, he looked like an old, broken man. He said he would never go to jail. His heart was bad and he didn't think he had long to live.

"Pepe Romano almost broke your neck when you sat on that bench in Plaza San Martin. He, too, knew that you were a newspaperman, and this was a hint and a rather vigorous one to mind your own business. It was bad enough for Romano to have myself and the rest of the police on his tail but with you around there was always the possibility that you might turn up something that we had overlooked. You know, each person has his own ideas, and given the same information, can come up with some startling conclusions. So you can see that Romano was beginning to regard you as an added thorn in his side."

Leon pulled a cigarette out of a package and shook it at me. He offered me one and I refused. I didn't want to come out of this big adventure with a pair of gassed lungs. "There is something else about which we have more substantial facts," he said. "Want to hear something priceless? This is really a gem. Remember the roughing up you got in the Barrio Rimac?"

"How could I forget that time," I said. "I still have a lump on my side where I caught a size twelve shoe."

Leon started to laugh and dabbed at his eyes with a handkerchief.

"What's so hilarious?" I demanded. "There's nothing amusing about being kicked half to death."

He put the handkerchief back into a pocket. "Listen to this. Moran had a fresh batch of customers in the line-up this morning and who do you think turned up?"

"Not Romano?" I asked. "Don't tell me they shot his double and Pepe was picked up for selling fake lottery tickets."

"They got your friend from the Barrio Rimac. The tall, skinny bird with the long legs and the dirty shirt."

"So what?" I said.

"His story was so good I'll have to tell it to my friends," said Leon. "Moran said he was almost on the floor when he heard it and said he hadn't laughed so much in years. Do you know what that bird told Moran? He was hired along with two other thugs by Romano to beat you up because you swindled him. Romano told the bum that you and he were partners on a lottery ticket that won 100,000 soles and that you had refused to come across with his share of the winnings. This disclosure hurt the nationalistic pride of the thugs, the idea of a foreigner doing such a thing, and they agreed to do what Romano wanted. No permanent injuries, mind you, but a good going over that would keep your mind occupied with other things for weeks. Of course, their pride was not sufficiently hurt to accept money for the job. Romano paid them each fifty soles and a couple of packages of American cigarettes. By the way, how about a loan?"

"Can't help your" I said. "Invested all of the loot in mining stocks."

"All right," said Leon. "I'll compromise. If you won't lend me any money, the least you can do is to buy me a drink."

"Come on," I said. "What are you waiting for?"

Leon took us to a place in Orrantia that was in a small block zoned for business, which also included a florist and a shop that sold Viennese pastries like *sachertorte,* which turned out to be a chocolate cake. Ted's Bar was started by an American pilot for one of the airlines and was managed by an Irishman from Santiago, whose name wasn't Ted. As far as I could determine, that wasn't the owner's name either. The spot was small and cozy but it had one bad mistake. There was a juke box in the corner which luckily was not in use and the place was quiet.

The bartender, who was also the Irishman from Santiago, put down a bottle of pisco from Moquegua and poured two glasses. The liquor was amber and tasted like the brandy it was supposed to be and not the paint solvent that was supposed to be the real thing.

"There's a few more things I'm wondering about," I said, "such as why Martellini had me write that letter. What do you think was in back of it?"

"That's a good point," said Leon. "Along with Romano, Martellini was uneasy about what you were doing standing in front of the shop. Pepe was in the store checking over a delivery of cocaine made by Professor Reimer when they spotted you looking in the window. Max had previously started to write a letter so they thought it would be a good idea to call you in and help finish it. They reasoned that you might say something about the investigation in the conversation that followed between you and Max. But, fortunately, you said little that would be balm for their nerves. Do you know that while you were writing the letter, and for some time afterwards until you left, Romano was sitting in a closet listening to the conversation? Pepe didn't want to be seen leaving the store by you, and the letter scheme was cooked up quickly. You can be sure that this letter was never mailed."

"How about the knife sticking in your back," I said. "The souvenir from the wrestling matches. Romano?"

"Right," he said. "The knife was not the kind you could buy in a store. It was homemade. There were no fingerprints on it. Pepe must have worn gloves. But he slipped up, anyway. The knife was made from a file and we traced it to his place. The brand name was still on it, and Pepe's company was an exclusive distributor for that particular trade-mark in the country."

The bartender filled the glasses again. "I know what's on your mind now," said Leon, "that little incident we had with the Reverend Clark in the catacombs. I'll bet he'll have all his friends gathered around him listening to the story when he gets back to England."

"Romano?"

"It could be nobody else," he said. "Romano knew more about Old Lima than any guide in the business. Funny, I even dug up a thesis Romano had written while at the University on the very subject. Too bad he had to get into a business he knew nothing about. The movie business. Nobody knows better than you how expensive that equipment is. Guess his ego got the best of him.

Anyway, the slab that hit the Reverend Clark was checked thoroughly for fingerprints. It was a mass of smudges probably made by the fellow who first put it into place, plus dirt and mold. It was impossible to get any clear prints from it. But the place and the method adds up to Romano. It was a wonderful opportunity to get the both of us at the same time, and if the Reverend Clark hadn't been in the way, he might have done it. Incidentally, the museum job was one that Pepe did not do. It was the result of negligence on the part of the workmen who were repairing the idol. They neglected to reinforce the statue properly. They should have put a framework of some kind around the thing but they were too lazy and settled for the two logs since they were returning in a few hours. The two ropes hanging from the logs had nothing to do with the crash. They just happened to be there. One of the workmen was even drunk when they came back. The three of them will have to work about a hundred years to pay for that big piece of stone."

"There is another item," I said. "The most important one of them all. If Lisa had an idea that Romano killed Barkovit, why didn't she go to the police?"

"That's easy," said Leon. "First of all, Barkovit could have been killed on his way to see Romano by any of several black market boys he had defrauded in bad deals. She wasn't sure. We know that they were out for his blood. Lisa did too. Only, we didn't think they would resort to murder. Lisa probably had other ideas. Secondly, Lisa and that snake Martellini, were attempting to blackmail Romano. She couldn't very well tell the police that she knew Romano killed Barkovit because he wouldn't cooperate in handing over the blackmail money."

Soon after Leon had left us, I found myself taking a long hard look at Elena.

"What are thinking about?" she asked seriously.

I answered slowly. "Something I've had on my mind for several days."

She raised her eyebrows questioningly, but her lips were smiling.

"That's right," I nodded. "A small motel in Miami Beach for almost five more weeks."

She tossed her ash-blonde hair and there was a twinkle in her gray eyes.

"And then?" she asked.

"Let's wait and find out," I said.

We finished our drinks and got up and left.